WITHDRAWN

MONTE CARLO

Also by Peter Terrin in English translation

The Guard (2012)
Post Mortem (2015)

PETER TERRIN

MONTE CARLO

Translated from the Dutch by
David Doherty

MACLEHOSE PRESS
QUERCUS · LONDON

First published in the Dutch language as *Monte Carlo* by
De Bezige Bij, Amsterdam, in 2014
First published in Great Britain in 2017 by

MacLehose Press
An imprint of Quercus Publishing Ltd
Carmelite House
50 Victoria Embankment
London EC4Y 0DZ

An Hachette UK company

"Space Oddity" written by David Bowie
Published by Onward Music Limited

The book was published with the support of the Flemish Literature Fund
(www.flemishliterature.be)

Flemish
Literature
Fund

A CIP catalogue record for this book is available
from the British Library.

ISBN (HB) 978 0 85705 437 1
ISBN (Ebook) 978 0 85705 438 8

10 9 8 7 6 5 4 3 2 1

Designed and typeset in Goudy Old Style by Libanus Press, Marlborough
Printed and bound in Great Britain by Clays Ltd, St Ives plc

For my son Willem

"Check ignition
and may God's love be with you."
– David Bowie, "Space Oddity"

1

The fire is not yet fire. Not quite. But the high-grade fuel that has just leaked from the Sutton is no longer liquid. It is, at this instant, changing form, a brutal transition accompanied by what some will describe as a roar – a cliché, as in fact it is the sound of a creature gasping for oxygen, an immense beast. Not yet fire but a colourless cloud of heat, invisible for now in the bright sunlight of this unseasonably warm spring day in Monte Carlo. A cloud that propels him forward and at the same time envelops him. Overalls, underwear, even the brilliantine in his hair are still precious barriers, affording him protection, sparing his skin. At this instant they exist side by side, in equilibrium, his overalls and the churning heat. The fire that is not yet fire.

2

The man's name is Jack Preston.

His father, a mild-mannered fellow who died for King and country, had wanted to name him Adam, but his mother thought Adam too genteel, a name above their station. Adam, she thought, leaning back into the plumped-up pillows, feeling her newborn son's lips close around the very sensitive nipple of her left breast and hearing him moan softly, as if from a surge of happiness after life's first ordeal, a happiness his little body could barely contain, so that the excess had to be carried away by successive tremors of his vocal chords. To call him Adam would elicit inappropriate expectations and predestine him for a life blighted by disillusion. And so he became Jack. After her stillborn younger brother who had not left her thoughts for a single moment in recent months, and who only the other night had appeared in her dream as a grown man and had shaken her by the hand, a handshake that left no doubt as to his identity.

Adam, his father thought eleven years later. The thought coincided with the impact of a bullet in the sand close to his face. Now that he was lying on this foreign beach with a wound to his chest, far beyond pain and no longer part of the tumult, his fear ebbed away. The mortar fire, the hoarse cries, the whistling bullets, the sea, all became a blur. In the moment at which the speeding bullet stirred up the sand and made a furrow directly in his line of sight, the name Adam came to him as a fond memory, an unexpected gift, the son his son also was. The silent pleasure of a secret

bond, contained in a single word. Adam. He whispered, felt
the movement of his lips and died.

3

The Prince is all smiles. The most important day of the year
is going entirely to plan. With the obligatory dinner behind
him and the social niceties concluded to his satisfaction,
he seeks the hand of his American wife, whose elegance
makes a prediction of the name her parents gave her.

The mood is agreeable, the company having grown accustomed to one another. Sunlight streams in through the vast
windows of the reception area, reflected by the distant azure
of the sea with a brilliance that verges on the audible. High
in the sky, a circling bird captures his attention as it glides
on the air currents and then turns against them, as if stitch-
ing with its sharp beak, loop after loop, an invisible tear
in the fabric of the firmament. The Prince becomes the
bird. He surveys this patch of land dashed against the flank
of a mountain and gazes eagle-like over God's shoulder
at the human activity, the concentration of effort, energy
and intellect, the illustrious accumulation of extraordinary
wealth and architecture, its allure amplified by the colour of
the rocks above and the blinding white of the neatly ranked

yachts in the marina below; this principality, he thinks, older and wiser and with a hint of nostalgia brought on by the wine, is an ongoing promise never to be fulfilled. And at its very heart, contours sharply drawn, the Grand Prix circuit. A twisting ring of electrifying absence.

He takes his wife's wedding ring between his fingers and utters the silent hope that no lives will be lost today, not like last year. With his other hand he smooths his moustache. The Prince then turns to face his guests, but in his thoughts he is with Deedee.

4

Jack Preston was thirteen when he began to tinker with the tractor over at Colin's farm. It was a Massey Ferguson from the early Thirties that stood in the shadow of one of the huge sheds built at right angles to the road. There were six sheds on either side, giving the road the appearance of a driveway that ran through Colin's land. Some had open sides to keep the hay dry. In the preceding two years Jack Preston had become a taciturn boy, ever since he had stood beside his mother and listened as a man from the army, holding his cap against the gleaming buttons of his uniform and staring over their heads into the hallway behind them, recited the message he had been ordered to deliver.

The tractor had been doomed to slowly rust, shot through with climbing weeds, a quiet place for the cats to shelter from the wind. It was a process to which Colin and his farmhands had resigned themselves, though none of them would have admitted it. Every farm had one – a tractor, a trailer, a muck cart, something that from a given moment never again left its spot, an object to which time could stick and stake its claim in a setting that was caught up in the turning of the seasons.

Jack would run over to the farm after school. Sometimes he would see no-one there for days on end and the looming, abandoned sheds frightened him so much that he murmured an Our Father as he concentrated on the job he had set himself. As yet he knew nothing of engines, could not begin to explain how they worked. He tinkered. He arranged the components of the dismantled engine one by one on a horse blanket. In search of replacements for worn seals, he explored the drawers of the workshop in the nearest shed. He polished with spit and rags. Each time he ventured a little deeper, memorising his way into the heart of the machine before fitting everything together as if slowly backing out of a room he had entered.

After three months, the engine of the Ferguson shone like new. The fact that it still did not run was of no great importance.

5

The fire is not yet fire and the people are waiting, heads peeping above the flowers on the little balconies of the tallest apartment blocks. They smoke, wait, lean over wrought-iron railings and gaze down onto boulevard Albert Premier and the packed grandstand at the starting grid. On the bend at the little church of Sainte-Dévote out towards avenue d'Ostende, men in white shirts are sitting on the stone balustrades. In the climb towards Beau Rivage, at the splashing fountain outside the famous casino, at Mirabeau and the dip into the hairpin bend, at the exit of the tunnel, the chicane, on the steps at the sharp corner by the Bureau de Tabac, along the majestic quayside, on the decks of countless yachts and up to the tight right turn from Gazomètre onto boulevard Albert Premier, everyone is waiting, keenly anticipating the cars that will soon be swarming like insects through the streets for eighty laps, cigar-shaped bodies suspended between four high wheels.

6

On the grandstand at the starting grid a woman takes a camera from her handbag. The man to her right has an uncouth air about him and forearms the size of thighs. Yet his wristwatch reveals that he is not out of place. He has not blundered onto this grandstand by mistake.

She lifts her handbag onto her lap, taking care not to touch him. The smoke from his cigarette is drifting in the opposite direction. He points at the cars on the starting grid and speaks in a loud voice to the man next to him. Then, as if to lend weight to his words, he plumps his densely haired forearm down on his leg, sending a ripple through the flesh of both limbs.

She could always change places with her husband, the man might not even notice, but she stays put for fear of offending him. To distract herself, she peers through the viewfinder of her camera.

His hair, his bearing – he could only be Italian. There is always something childish about a fat man, she thinks, even if his beard sprouts at his eye sockets and burrows deep under his shirt. Even if they smoke cigars and communicate in nothing but recalcitrant grunts, his type always fall for women who will mother them.

She thinks all this, not with distaste but with something closer to physical astonishment, imagining what it must be like, with him between the sheets. This unexpected sensation causes her to hide her face behind the camera.

Her husband does not know what she is thinking. She is taking photographs. No-one knows what she is thinking. She is a woman taking photographs, sitting on a grandstand next to a fat, Italian-looking man.

7

What sparked the news or how it spread, no-one can say. The chain of communication can no longer be traced and fades to irrelevance as soon as the name is spoken. Deedee. Everyone knows she is in Monaco. Everyone feels her presence. They understand this happening of which they are a part and reconcile themselves for one afternoon to the casual ease of the extraordinary. Deedee. A fêted young actress with the world at her feet, of course she is here. Her name, on the tip of every tongue, connects them all in a second circuit.

Deedee.

Cool as the flamed-marble hallways through which she is escorted to her suite. A provocative curl on her lips, even as chastely she lowers her gaze. A devout country girl who has gradually grown into the contours of the name by which everyone knows her. A duet with a brilliant *chansonnier*. An appearance on La Croisette in Cannes. Her blonde hair and the inexplicable way it embellishes her features; young women everywhere want a hairdo like it, an ambition that will make a laughing stock of many of them. Deedee. The insurrectionary students in Paris deride and desire her.

8

Always the left door first, then the right. Jack Preston dragged them along the rail and slid the padlock through the eyes where they met in the middle. Colin had offered to rent him the shed for next to nothing. Jack was seventeen and he was earning a living. Maintenance mostly, the odd repair job. Having dug an oil-change pit and put together an orderly workbench, he tended to the farmer's tractors and cars belonging to the villagers, Ford owners almost to a man. He turned the padlock and clicked it shut: that simple sound, feeling the weight of the lock leave his hands and letting it hang on the towering doors, it had the solemnity of a seal. The late sun turned the corn orange, the swallows twittered and he tapped a cigarette from the pack he kept in the breast pocket of his overalls. He wore the black smears on his hands with pride and held his fingers as if they were incapable of movement, the fingers of a manly hand. But in church his hands were like a child's, clasped in prayer. He scraped his soles on the iron boot scraper before entering the little wooden porch, which smelled of disinfectant, marvelling yet again at how shoes had worn away the stone of the church's threshold, at how – in time – the impossible became possible. Here he was, seventeen, money and cigarettes in his pocket and the key to his own lock-up. He bowed his head in thanks and prayed for his mother. He closed his eyes, heard the sound of his own breathing and prayed for his dear mother, who in four months' time would find her rest in the Lord, a sudden, painless death, her heart in pieces.

9

Through the viewfinder of her camera the woman sees a man with brilliantine in his hair pull a length of duct tape from the roll. Another man looks on with his chin tucked into his chest, watching as his workmate crouches between the front and back wheels of the Sutton at the end of the front row of cars closest to her. Taking the edge between his teeth, the man with the tape tears off a strip and sticks it to the bodywork. The fat, Italian-looking man beside her is first to react. Out of the corner of her eye she sees his hairy forearm abruptly leave its resting place on his thigh and just as she grasps the connection between the rising, pointing arm and the length of black tape obscuring the top half of the image in the middle of the bodywork, she hears her husband moan. Her husband is a reserved man, a man of business, a property broker with connections in the world of Formula One – connections about which she hears nothing specific and about which she does not enquire, in accordance with the unspoken agreements that keep matrimonial relations running smoothly – yet now she distinctly hears him utter a moan of disappointment, of disbelief, and feels a rush of indignation at the shameless ambush of this unthinkable, almost theatrical sound, albeit not half as theatrical as the arm of the fat, Italian-looking man. Through the viewfinder she continues to look at the image on the Sutton, until a second strip of tape hides it from view. A sailor. Yes, she clearly saw the head of a sailor. A roar of laughter from the fat man punches a hole in the dignified serenity of the grandstand. There is the odd flurry of disapproval, but the overriding mood is one of amusement, protest mixed with amusement, the tumult builds and the man with the roll of tape takes a bashful look over his shoulder, unsettled perhaps by the response he has triggered. The black tape has obscured a noble, three-quarter portrait of a sailor with a ginger beard, framed by a lifebelt entwined in rope. The word "Player's" is still legible above, the words "Navy Cut" below. Ginger beard, red lettering. A brand of cigarettes.

10

Applause resounds as the Prince takes his place in the royal box. Before he is quite seated, his son clambers onto his lap, trapping his foot – his heel, to be precise – between the sturdy chair legs. The Prince raises one hand in the air, only for a moment and no higher than his head, to acknowledge the crowd's reception and at the same time to emphasise that today is not about him, nor about his wife and children. He takes a firm hold of his son, this is hardly appropriate behaviour for a boy his age, and having extricated his foot, he straightens the boy's white linen jacket with a fatherly tug and orders him to sit on his own chair.

At the start of the race, the Prince and his loved ones will take shelter behind the glass barrier. Only ten minutes to go in the lead-up to that explosion of horsepower. He surveys the field, insofar as he is able, the chosen few of the *beau monde* strolling amiably among the drivers who are giving one final interview, among the racing cars and the mechanics, team bosses and press photographers, through the shadows cast by the trees that line the boulevard. No sign of Deedee, although he knows that she plans to go for a walkabout under escort. She is as young as his wife was when they first met. She reminds him of his wife as a girl, has the same sovereign vulnerability. He *knows* her, Deedee. When he speaks to her in a little while, it should be with her hands in his, not as a father but with the open-hearted charm of an older man, *hors concours*, a man who does not compete with other men and who is capable of seducing her as naturally as she has seduced his principality.

11

Two days before the Grand Prix, Jack Preston is in one of the city's side streets helping to unload the Sutton 44 from its lorry. He is not sure what to make of his new overalls. Alfie and Jim, walking around in the self-same outfit, are equally perplexed. With every movement of his arms and legs he sees himself, and feels like a bit of a clown clad in red and gold. It is only when the car rolls from the back of the lorry that the penny drops. First comes the familiar sight of the long exhaust pipes of the three-litre V.8 Ford Cosworth engine, a startling innovation in the car's construction. But then comes the bodywork, no longer traditional green with the yellow stripe down the middle that encircles the air inlet at the nose. Jack, as everyone looking on, is dumbstruck. Their team boss, Blackman, has pulled another rabbit out of the hat. The car is red and white, its nose finished in gold. Team Sutton is now emblazoned GOLD LEAF TEAM SUTTON and on either side of the driver's cockpit the bodywork bears the familiar logo of a cigarette brand! Cigarettes? On a Formula One car? Firestone, Esso, Dunlop, B.P., that goes without saying, thinks Jack, they supply the oil and fuel and tyres, but what business does a brand of cigarettes have being there? The product doesn't fit the context. Alfie looks at Jack with an expression that mixes merriment with disbelief. The team they work for is different from the rest. How had their boss persuaded Gold Leaf to take the plunge? Where did he get the nerve to ditch Britain's traditional racing green just like that? And what the hell was a sailor doing on a Formula One racing car?

12

It happens by accident. The woman has been holding the camera for some time, peering through the viewfinder now and again, taking the occasional snap. But now she waits, realising that the film is almost full, that she probably has only one photograph left. She wants to wait for the right moment, yet later she will not be able to recall taking the final shot. The fuel is no longer liquid, the transition is taking place. She remembers the heat hitting her face, an invisible cloud, the fire not yet fire. It is a picture that would be impossible to take knowingly; the event has recorded itself. Sitting on the grandstand beside the fat, Italian-looking man, camera poised for one last shot, the woman clicks without meaning to and unwittingly takes the only photograph of this moment, a coincidence within a coincidence. She will remember nothing about it. Nothing save the heat hitting her face.

13

For four years Jack worked as head mechanic for a team that competed in the British Rally Championship. It was a responsibility he took very seriously and, although he did not show it, he enjoyed the respect he commanded from young and old, both on the rally circuit and back home in the village. Three days before his thirty-third birthday, the postman delivered a letter that nailed him to the spot. There it was in black and white, below the green-and-yellow Sutton logo. His wife tugged gently at his arm and asked him what was the matter. He looked into the indefinable colour of her eyes. His wife, her pale lashes, slender shoulders and broad hips, her hands red and chapped. What could he say to help her understand this moment? Where to start? With Queen Elizabeth, who sixteen years earlier at Silverstone attended the very first Grand Prix of the brand-new Formula One World Championship? With Fangio, Farina and Moss, and the monstrous Ferrari and Maserati engines mounted on the front of their racing cars? Or perhaps with what the Italians had disparagingly dubbed the "garagistas", the teams who had completely changed the face of Formula One ten years in? Teams like Cooper and Sutton and Brabham, all British-based, each and every one housed in the hangars of disused World War II airfields, "garages" with plenty of tarmac for testing. Teams who deftly side-stepped the competition with the major engine manufacturers and focused on the car itself, its design, its weight, positioning a compact, energy-efficient engine behind the driver to achieve not only far superior roadholding but also to burn less rubber – a revolution that signalled the advent of modern-day Formula One . . . Yes, that was where to start, with the kind of team that he, Jack Preston, would be working for. That was the message he held in his hands, there in black and white. It thrilled him and it made him tremble. That evening he went to church and lit a candle.

14

Even before he takes the tape between his teeth and tears off the first strip he can feel the eyes of the spectators on his back. Those eyes are everywhere and on a Grand Prix weekend even the mechanics do not escape their notice. Along with the drivers and the cars, they too are worth watching, and while no-one has come especially to see them, they become part of the spectacle: the men who get to touch those insanely expensive racing machines. You have to be made of stern stuff to withstand that added pressure, even if no-one knows exactly what it is you do. This is an opportunity reserved for only the best mechanics, another thing the spectators do not stop to consider. Every mechanic on the starting grid has more than earned his stripes and it is a humiliation to be out there wielding a lowly roll of duct tape. They looked at one another when Blackman broke the news and gave the order, but Alfie and Jim were longer-serving members of the team and so Jack Preston, the oldest of the three at thirty-five, picked up the roll of tape without a word and made his way over to the Sutton 44. Alfie followed him out for moral support. Once the first strip is in place, something happens up in the stands. A man guffaws, a deep, emphatic burst of laughter intended to draw attention to Jack and the tape. A daring move is being laughed off the stage, cheering the Automobile Federation's ruling, prompted by the B.B.C. and I.T.V., to stop teams turning their racing cars into hoardings on wheels, a step too far. Though Blackman succeeded in having the ruling overturned during yesterday's qualifying sessions, today it is his turn to bite the dust. Yet up in the stands, other sounds are stirring, sounds that condemn the ban as a reactionary, knee-jerk response. As Jack Preston sticks a second strip over the sailor's face – his nose almost touching the red, white and gold – he feels the conflict in his own chest. All of a sudden he is the centre of attention, soon camera crews will come rushing over to film him covering up the sailor, and he is reminded once again that this work calls for a particular mindset and he is surprised – surprised and proud – that apparently he has what it takes, that ultimately this is where he belongs, in this team with its sights set firmly on the future, a team experimenting behind closed doors, testing wings designed not to send the car soaring but to press it to the track so it can corner faster than the rest.

15

Jack Preston has followed Blackman's orders and covered up the image on either side of the Sutton. The commotion in the stands has died down following the applause that greeted the Prince and his family. Alfie and Jim have begun their final checks. It feels like the very height of summer on this warm day in May. The car is radiating the heat it has absorbed, too hot to be touched without gloves. Jerry Stark runs a hand through his thick black hair, dons his helmet and buckles it under his chin. A short distance away, MacLaren and Gill are having a *tête-à-tête*, Thompson stands beside them, still recovering from his crash six weeks earlier in a Formula Two race and looking a little lost in his civvies, the accident had been his own fault, plain for all to see. Blackman brings his face to within inches of Stark's and says something he evidently wants to share with his driver alone, a final word of encouragement, a reminder about a particular turn, how to create an opportunity to overtake on this notoriously tricky circuit. The buzz of activity on the starting grid is building to a climax. Everyone knows Deedee is on her way, the drivers stand proud and put off climbing into their cockpits. What follows is one of those strange moments when, anticipating what they know is coming, all those involved in the race, from the starting grid to the stands along boulevard Albert Premier, fall silent one by one, even the Prince. Sensing that others have stopped talking, people go quiet themselves and an abrupt and improbable hush ripples through the crowd. Words are swallowed in the certainty that something is brewing and people hear the noiseless rush, quicker than fire, so impressive that they fall silent with an instinctive reverence, at once forgetting what they were saying, wanting only to listen with the rest until, in those few seconds when their silence is absolute and people listen to distant sounds together as if dumbstruck, it turns out simply to be one of those moments that sometimes take hold of a crowd but signify nothing, and everyone is free to speak again. Meanwhile, Jack Preston is preoccupied with heat and air resistance and how the two might conspire to peel back the tape during the race and leave Stark speeding around Monte Carlo with strips flapping off the Sutton 44, an even greater affront than racing with tape on the car in the first place. He sticks double vertical strips over the edges of his handiwork, leaving an ugly black square on the bodywork, large enough to conceal a hole the driver could stick his hand through. He repeats the process on the other side of the car, the stand side, and it is then that Jack Preston picks up the scent for the first time. Amid the perfume of spring and asphalt and people and machines and excitement and rubber and God only knows what else, amid the atmosphere so typical of the final countdown to a Grand Prix, he smells fuel. It is a fleeting, half-conscious thought, a flicker that vanishes from his mind as he proceeds to reproduce his black square on the car's left flank, and the tape he tears off with his teeth leaves a nasty taste in his mouth as a new sensation shivers through the crowd, one that does not impose silence, not this time. It is as if a magnetic field is sweeping across the boulevard, the stands and the balconies, a force no-one can escape as they turn their heads towards the same tantalising spot, though Deedee is not yet visible to most of them. They do not fall silent but go on talking, almost compulsively, without listening to one another or hearing their own words, in search of a demeanour, a dignified pose, as they sense her proximity. She and her entourage must have entered the circuit somewhere along the quayside.

Photojournalists, newshounds and cameramen crowd in on her and are shoved aside by her bodyguards. People call out to her from the stands. Shyly, she chats to a few of the drivers, the seriousness with which she listens as they talk about their cars never lasting long, making way for a captivating smile that intimates her desire to move on. She ruffles her hair, brushes back stray locks or sweeps them aside with a brisk toss of her head to expose her long neck, every movement as artless and unassuming as a young girl shrugging off sleep in the early morning. Slowly, she makes her way towards the starting line. Gill – who else? – takes advantage of the occasion and kisses her on the cheek, much to the merriment of the onlookers; Gill who at a party last year donned women's clothes and stilettos and danced on tables until he came to grief on the broken stem of a wine glass. He kisses her cheek, but Deedee's eyes sparkle as if she has received the attentions of a true gentleman. Jack Preston catches a glimpse of her amid the scrum of backs and legs, and the woman up in the stands is poised, her face half hidden behind her camera, only one frame left on the roll, and the smell of fuel intensifies but does not register because, at that moment, Deedee does something strange.

She looks at him.

He is sure of it.

Among the jostling heads and cameras, she fixes him with her gaze. He is standing quite alone beside the Sutton 44 and she looks at him. Gesturing impatiently, she seeks a gap among the throng of bodies, reaches out, bobs under their arms and slips through. Laughing, she breaks free of her entourage and walks to the side of the boulevard, long, loping strides in his direction: the casual ease of the extraordinary on this afternoon in the streets of Monte Carlo. She recognises him, she must have seen him in Spain or last year at Monza or Francorchamps, though he cannot remember her being there. He would have known. Yet she must have seen him at work somewhere because she recognises him, breaks free and comes towards him, in full view of the spectators. His heart leaps and, because he knows her face so well, it feels like a genuine reunion and he readies himself for a handshake, an embrace, a kiss perhaps, from the other side of the Sutton. This moment lasts no longer than a stride or two, timed to the sway of her hips. Realisation comes in a flash as, out of the corner of his eye, he sees that the news-hounds, astonished and amused by her sudden escape, are paying him no heed but are turning and breaking into a sprint. And it dawns on Jack Preston that Deedee is not looking *at* him but *past* him, eyes set on but one goal and, although he cannot see it, he knows the Prince has risen

31

from his seat and is descending the steps of the royal box. Reading the signs – the turning heads, Deedee's unwavering gaze, the newshounds ignoring him – he understands that, sweeping etiquette and protocol aside, she has chosen this route only as a spontaneous and unimpeded approach, the path of least resistance between the Sutton 44 and the grandstand, on her way to the Prince. That's the kind of woman she is and that is why everyone loves her. The photographers hare along the path Deedee has abandoned, the shortest route to the royal box, and as she reaches the left rear wheel of the Sutton the sound erupts, between one footfall and the next, the sound of an immense creature gasping for oxygen, the fire not yet fire, a colourless cloud of heat, invisible for now in the bright sunlight: it propels Jack Preston forward, envelops him, and the woman up in the stands unwittingly clicks the shutter. At that exact moment, when his overalls and the brilliantine in his hair are still barriers, existing in equilibrium with the churning heat, he reaches out his arm and snatches Deedee away, shields her body with his. They are blown against the hoardings, his cheek pressed to hers, his scream drowning her scream. The white-shirted men with their rolled-up sleeves leaning on the railings at Sainte-Dévote make out a distant commotion, hear the gasp of the beast and see a black plume of smoke form some thirty feet above Stark's Sutton. They can only guess as to its cause, but they see a thick black plume of smoke rising above boulevard Albert Premier and below it a red flame surging at the heart of what must surely be a raging inferno.

ALDSTEAD

16

It would not be long in coming. Some things in life cannot remain without consequences. What Jack Preston had done and, in his own words, had survived with God's help, was one of those things. No two ways about it.

This realisation filled him with great excitement, his emotions fought for precedence. In the morning, the desire for what the future would bring had the upper hand. In the evening, as the Mediterranean light dimmed and the hospital corridors grew quiet, fear gradually took hold. For days on end his blood would not settle. The nurses were amazed at how calmly this man withstood the pain; morphine scarcely had to be administered.

In addition, the Englishman was polite and modest, a cooperative patient. During his weeks at the hospital in Nice, they never once heard him complain about his condition. Nor about the discomfort of having to sleep on his stomach and being bound at the ankles and knees to stop him turning over. Nor about the impossibility of sitting down on a chair or a toilet, due to the burns that reached from the crown of his head to the curve of his behind.

The matron believed her patient was capable of such fortitude because he had looked death in the face. This enabled him to put everything into perspective, so that he refused to be disheartened by the fact that he was irrevocably disfigured.

17

Confirmation came in the shape of a journalist. The man was announced by Marie, the shortest of the nurses, the kind-eyed girl who spoke a little English. Although it had taken the journalist a while to track him down – five days had passed since the incident – it was not yet possible for Jack Preston to get out of bed. The prospect of having his picture taken with stubble on his cheeks appalled him more than revealing the distressing position in which he found himself, lying in a metal cage over which sheets were draped, his feet and head sticking out of either end. At the same time he realised that this image would speak volumes to the readers of what, if it were not a newspaper, must surely be a popular weekly magazine.

The journalist sat down on the chair that Marie had slid into Jack's field of vision. Jack would have liked to get a better idea of the kind of man he was dealing with, but in the course of the brief conversation he was unable to summon the courage to ask the journalist to tilt his head for a moment to an angle where his cheek might be resting on an adjacent pillow, so that they could look each other in the eye. He assumed that the journalist must be top notch, in great demand, so overworked in fact that he could not find the time to take his suit to the cleaners and was obliged whenever possible to make appointments in a simple but respectable café close to his apartment – or at least that would explain the odour that his presence caused to spread throughout the room. The way his sunglasses were perched tiara-like on his head, keeping his long and unwashed hair out of his eyes, was perhaps evidence of a growing trend among members of the press to explore their Bohemian side.

18

Marie sat at the head of the bed. Jack was not able to see her face, but he could see her hands, which for the entire duration of the conversation lay unmoving in her lap, as if they did not belong to her. In spite of her dogged concentration, the interview was awkward. The journalist's rambling sentences were reduced to a couple of key words in English. Before long, this gave rise to a conversation within a conversation, one that sounded more like an altercation, held in another kind of French. Marie tried to stay calm, but judging by the steadily lengthening intervals that followed his questions, she was irritated by the man's condescending attitude. In an effort to help her, Jack Preston spoke slowly and gave a well-ordered account of the events.

At a certain moment, the journalist shook his head. He tucked his notebook into his inside pocket and hunched forward, arms resting on his knees. Then he leaned back, crossed his legs and let one arm drop behind the back of the chair in exasperation, while Marie continued her search for the translation of a word he had repeated several times, at first in a genuine attempt to get to the bottom of things, then frustrated and angry and, finally, incomprehensibly cynical.

From the vague explanation he received from Marie, Jack Preston identified the word as one he had already used. "Bodyguard?" The journalist jabbed a pointing finger at him, nodding excitedly, and said "You! You!" He acted out someone leaping into the path of a speeding bullet. A bodyguard.

Jack repeated what he had already said. Perhaps Marie had misunderstood him the first time. Perhaps she had skipped crucial details. There was little more he could say about the bodyguard. When the pressure in the pipeline had dropped and the fuel from the Sutton was no longer shooting directly at them, the bodyguard had dragged Deedee and then him away from the fire and over to the royal box. He did not know the man's name.

As far as Jack could tell with his cheek resting on the pillow, once Marie had stopped talking the journalist appeared to be impressed by what he had heard. He broke his silence with a deep sigh and without another word he stood and shook Marie by the hand, giving a barely perceptible shake of the head that spoke of incredulity. He blinked briefly at Jack Preston by way of farewell.

19

It was late afternoon when it hit him. Since the journalist had left that morning, Jack Preston had been unable to shake the feeling that he had overlooked something, an element that was important for the article. Now he realised the omission was not his own but the journalist's: a photograph . . .

By this time Marie had gone home, and to speak to another nurse on the subject, one with an even more tenuous grasp of English, struck him as a futile undertaking.

He pricked up his ears at the sound of every footstep in the long corridor. It was far from improbable that the journalist, too, had discovered his oversight and was now doing everything in his power to pay a second visit to the hospital before the evening was out. As the time ticked by, this notion became a premonition.

Hours passed and the quiet settled in. He could pick out the sounds made by the door down the corridor, through which every visitor had to pass. The muted groan of the mechanism that pushed the door back into its frame with a series of short jerks, culminating in an unexpectedly loud final chord. After eight, even the tightening of the internal spring when the door opened did not escape his notice; each time he heard it he was sure it had been set in motion by the journalist rushing in.

The next day, once she had cleared away his breakfast, Marie crouched at arm's length beside his bed and looked at him inquisitively with her bright eyes. And as he began to speak, it occurred to him that a journalist was not a photographer. How could he have been so slow to catch on? No journalist worth his salt would take his own photographs. The magazine would send a professional photographer, someone with an eye for light and colour. A craftsman.

Half apologising, he attempted to share his insight with Marie. She listened to him with a charming smile that remained in place even after he had stopped talking. After a pause, she tried to clarify something about the photographer. He interrupted her, his mind clearer than it had been a moment earlier. She must excuse him for his short-sightedness; of course he understood that his health came first and that it was up to the medical staff to decide when he was well enough for the hospital to invite the magazine to conduct a photoshoot.

20

Maureen paid him a single visit. Blackman paid for her trip and the hotel.

She entered the room as timidly as she had boarded an aeroplane for the first time five hours before. She kissed her husband and then, unable to say a word, kissed him again. Her lips were dry and flaky, and her nose glowed as if she had a streaming cold. Her husband asked her not to cry, not anymore, words which robbed her of the last of her self-control. She burst into sobbing, her head bowed and her whole body huddled around the monogrammed, lace-edged handkerchief that she pressed to her nose with both hands. She was standing several feet away from him.

He pushed himself up, wriggled out from under the cage and slid from the bed. To be sure, he held both her hands tight for a moment and said, "Don't touch my back." Then he embraced his wife, Maureen Coxwold, a seamstress from the neighbouring village, daughter of a contractor with three vans and a lorry, who had become a customer of his through Colin the farmer.

A little later she sat with her knees together, drinking a cup of coffee. He showed her the progress he had made, what he did when the rest of the hospital slept and he, to use his own words, had a little word with the Lord. He knelt in front of her and slowly lowered his backside until it was resting on his heels. He relaxed his shoulders and joked that this was a kind of sitting too.

Maureen did not laugh.

From where he was kneeling he saw her buttocks tense against the edge of the chair. Supporting himself on her thighs he stood again. It took a conscious effort to banish the lustful thoughts from his mind.

21

No-one else came to visit in the weeks that followed. Jack Preston nevertheless felt better, much better. He walked patiently through the corridors of the hospital, feeling secure in his temporary surroundings. Every so often he caught glimpses of himself as a stranger, more mummy than man. This was what a comic-strip hero looked like after hurtling into a ravine. But his face was not bandaged. A photograph could have been taken, one in which he was clearly recognisable. As night fell over the beautiful landscape, he posed in front of the darkening windows.

It was possible that they had run the story with a photograph of Deedee. Magazine readers had an insatiable appetite for images of Deedee, even more so since the spectacular accident in Monte Carlo. They wanted pictures to prove that she really had escaped without so much as a scratch, that she had emerged miraculously from the savage blaze on the Grand Prix starting grid with only a few of her blonde hairs singed. She was the star, the girl they all knew. A shot of Deedee being comforted by the Prince of Monaco on the steps of the royal box – how could a mummified mechanic from Aldstead compete with that?

22

The thirty-seven days Jack Preston had spent in the hospital in Nice had given him plenty of time to think. What he knew of the reported facts disappointed him. From a number of comments made by Marie and a touching letter from Maureen, he had gleaned that not he but Deedee's bodyguard was being hailed as a hero. As the world looked on, this man had "pulled Deedee from the flames". In vain he tried to find out if his own part in the rescue had figured in the story, if his name had been mentioned anywhere.

This disappointment did not weigh heavily on his mood.

He was counting on Deedee. In a strange way, the partial misunderstanding elated him. The stream of inaccuracies in the press was bound to upset her. Before long she would be in touch and with heartfelt gratitude she would reveal to the world the true identity of the man who had saved her from the flames on boulevard Albert Premier.

23

There was nothing else for it. An aeroplane with special facilities was too expensive, Blackman reckoned, and even a standard ambulance cost a small fortune. No-one was handier with an oxy welder than Alfie. Early one afternoon he adapted one of the Sutton vans so that Jack Preston could travel back to England lying on his stomach.

In the back of the van, Jack felt like a precious instrument among all the other instruments, an integral part of the team. That feeling grew stronger after the first stop at a filling station, when the nurse travelling with him went to sit in the front next to the driver, a sturdy young man who had introduced himself as Alfie's neighbour's nephew. Later he would tell the story to his friends, to his wife and children, a story no-one would believe. But it was true. On an improvised bed in the back of a van, he had brought Jack Preston back to Aldstead.

The nurse had served in World War II and looked as if she did not scare easily. For miles on end Jack had averted his eyes from the rolls of skin that sagged like stockings around her ankles.

She was thorough and brisk, just what one might expect of a seasoned nurse. The pain he felt when she attended to his wounds on the ferry was more intense yet at the same time more bearable than the pain he would experience in the days that followed, when Maureen took over the care of her husband. With the nurse, his chest swelled and he felt the life fizz in his veins, but with his wife the pain left him hunched and panting like a lap dog. Ever more carefully, ever more slowly, humming a tune to distract him, Maureen wound the bandages around her forefinger and middle finger until at last she reached the layer that lay directly over his burns, the layer that after twelve hours had become a part of his body, a tender, newly acquired skin.

24

She had waited for him on the toll bridge, out of sight of the rest of the village.

"You're home." Tenderly she brushed the tip of her nose against his cheek. They stood between the open doors at the back of the van. "You're home," she whispered.

The toll bridge was the main route into the village. No toll had been paid for six years, ever since the last tollman had blundered drunk into the water one night and, finding no purchase on the slippery slope, had drifted slowly down to the riverbed, weighted by the bulging coin-belt around his waist.

The other way in was further north, a pointed medieval bridge that spanned a kink in the river where the rushing water cut deep into the stone before slowing on its way to the broad estuary. The old bridge, almost eight miles from the village, was used only by a few sheep farmers from over the way who herded their flocks to the lean pastures up on the rise.

Almost every car that drove across the toll bridge was bound for Aldstead and announced its arrival with a thunderous rattling of beams. The rock face of the rise towered above the houses and acted like a hand cupped to an ear. At night, no-one could cross the water unnoticed.

The village straggled along a single street. Approached from one end, the first building to come into view was its only pub, the Black Swan. Anyone coming from the other direction was greeted by the church, set some sixteen feet above the road, a striking, sombre shape that seemed to look off into the distance, surrounded by a ramshackle collection of rust-brown stones and crosses and flanked by two tall cypresses of the darkest green, where the sparrows bickered in the morning.

25

The early summer weather had reached Aldstead too. The air was hot and muggy, yet the smell of winter lingered in the kitchen of the cottage. Maureen had thrown the windows open to no perceptible effect. To welcome him, to comfort him, she had made shepherd's pie, his favourite, a dish he hadn't had a hope of eating in Nice.

She had been planning this meal ever since she had packed her case to visit him. A casual remark at the hospital had been enough to strengthen her resolve and since then she had cherished her resolution like the little gold crucifix that lay against her breastbone and that she turned between her fingers when she was lost in thought.

When he pricked his fork into the crust of mashed potato and reached the mince beneath, the steam hit him in the face. She said she had taken the dish out of the oven at least an hour ago. After three mouthfuls, beads of sweat appeared on his forehead. She sat opposite him at the wooden table and said the meal could wait. He said it was just the way he liked it. For the first time in his life, her husband winked at her.

It was too warm to smoke. In the shadow of one of the cypresses he crushed half a cigarette in the grass under the ball of his foot. He scraped the mud from his shoes and stepped hastily through the stifling heat of the wooden porch into the cool of the church.

Jack Preston lit a candle for his mother, glad that she had been spared the sight of him in his present state; then he lit a candle for his father, who grew ever dimmer in his memories, reduced to the man who, on days like today, had chased him around the garden with ice-cold water from the well. Once he had said his prayers, his gaze rested on the statue of the Blessed Virgin Mary and he jumped when he heard the name Deedee echo through the nave, having escaped from his own lips.

The silence he had broken seemed irreparable.

26

Neither of them fully understood what happened, that first night in bed.

Ordinarily she would put her arms around him.

Ordinarily she would pull him to her; sometimes they kissed, mostly they withdrew quickly into their own sensations; he pressed his face to her pillow and saw images, she tilted her head back a little and stared at the beams on the ceiling; he smothered his breathing, she let out muted squeals.

Now she could not put her arms around him. What happened next came as a great surprise to her.

It was all because of her hands. She did not want to simply leave them lying on the sheet, as if she were rejecting him rather than encouraging him. The mere thought that she might give him that impression filled her with an old self-hatred at her own bashfulness. Once he was inside her, Maureen placed her hands on her husband's buttocks, just below the curve at the top of his legs where they slope inwards a little. It was all because of her hands, her hands on his buttocks.

Without her doing anything, her hands just resting there, only moving when he moved, it seemed to Jack as if Maureen were urging him on.

Surprised, he dug his elbows into the mattress and lifted his head from her pillow. Supporting himself with his arms, he looked into her eyes, which looked back unblinkingly. His gaze drifted downwards and, feeling her hands all the while, he watched the melting motion beneath him, a sluggish response to the rhythm of his thrusts, in the late light of the longest day of the year.

Overwhelmed, she tensed her hands and her grip on his buttocks tightened, so it seemed as if she were urging him to go faster still. The fire was stoked to unprecedented levels and, overcome, her fingertips found a place where they had never touched him before.

There was no time for squeals. All at once she found herself far beyond everything, in a boundless expanse she had never known existed. Breathless, she waited to return to herself.

A little later she cried silent tears of joy, now that she had found a possible explanation for her years of childlessness.

He lay with his cheek on the pillow and stared out at the deepening blue. Dazed, he could think only of his wife and wonder what in God's name had got into her.

27

Between the sheds on Colin's farm, the swallows chased one another with piercing squawks that could be taken for passion or play. In the distance, beneath the cloud of dust that rose on the far side of the hill, he heard the harmonies of engines, a high-pitched chorus of agricultural machinery. Billy kept watch over the farmyard. Stretching his long chain to its limit, he had already plucked the familiar scent from the air and, with broad sweeps of his bushy tail, he waited until Jack Preston came into view and approached, before barking once and rolling around on his back to receive his affectionate greeting.

When Jack dragged the left door along the rail, a glimpse of the recent past escaped from his orderly workshop; the displacement of air and the light angling in set time back into motion. His first step stirred the same feeling that had struck him the previous day at the toll bridge, a sense that something had changed, albeit imperceptibly. The life he had lived no longer existed, the life before he left for Monte Carlo, when he had hung these tools in their place and sealed them with a padlock. It all looked identical, each and every banal object, yet it was no longer his, not really.

28

He opened the order book and examined the jobs on the list. His thoughts drifted to the post office in Little Habton, the neighbouring village almost seven miles south of Aldstead on the near side of the river. He considered driving there. It couldn't hurt to show his face, to remind everyone at the post office of recent events, so that any unusual item of post would not be unthinkingly returned to sender on the grounds that its like had never before been delivered to Aldstead.

Facing the wall on which screwdrivers and spanners hung in neat rows according to size, he sensed a presence over by the oil pit. Faster than the impulse to turn around, he realised who it was. He stood still, waiting for the slightest movement and then spun to face Ronny. The "boo" with which the boy had wanted to startle Jack came too late and seemed rather an expression of his own surprise: a bewildered echo of the "boo" Jack had not shouted. Laughing, the boy looked up through the cobwebs at a corner where the wall met the rafters.

Ronny almost always avoided eye contact. His ears and his feet stuck out to the side and the soft hair on his upper lip would never toughen to make a man of him, as it would any normal boy. His mother never left the house and people said it was a woman in the village who combed his black hair into the same neat white parting each morning. "Jack . . . is back," he said three times in a row, establishing the fact of Jack's return in a loud, coarse voice that contrasted with his drooping shoulders. His words clumped together in twos or threes at the back of his throat until – the pressure visible in his eyes and neck – they were suddenly released, strung on a short, urgent sigh.

29

Intellect aside, the defect that Ronny had borne since birth was most keenly present in his face. Under the eastern slant of his eyes and his small nose, it was his mouth, dispropor-tionately large and always open, that attracted the attention.

His thick, wet lower lip curled towards his chin, and even over his upper lip the boy had no control to speak of. It was something Jack Preston had never been able to get used to: the boy's whitish gums with their yellowish stumps that seemed to have chosen their position at random, his speckled tongue always in motion and too big to rest in his mouth, hence its tendency to loll and moisten his lower lip when there was no need.

Ronny was kind-hearted and quick to laugh, and everyone felt sorry for the boy. Not long after he was born, his father – a slight man with baleful eyes, made more penetrating by the black dust of the mines – had left without a word to anyone.

Ronny set off early in the morning and returned home to his mother only at bedtime. He sometimes roamed through the surrounding fields or up on the rise, dozing among the sheep, drinking from the water put out for the cattle. But mostly he stuck to the village and the company of his fellow humans.

No-one could remember quite how it began, but from an early age Ronny would call in at every home. Strolling unannounced through the front or back door, he would pull up a chair or remain standing. No-one took umbrage at the boy, not even when he peered into their saucepans, interrupted their conversations or stood immobile in the middle of the floor so that the lady of the house had to mop around him. His visits might last five minutes or an hour, but he always left abruptly, never a goodbye though always a smile, as he closed the door behind him and heeded the urge to wander. Off he would go, to rummage around in the little gardens, or to sit on the curb and chide himself out loud.

Maureen was in the habit of giving him something sweet to eat. While the boy's gaping mouth chomped on biscuits or a slice of cake, she would take his hand and hold it in her lap. When she went on to say what a handsome lad he was, with his lovely black hair, Jack Preston – on the rare occasions when he witnessed such a scene – could expect Ronny to shoot him a triumphant look.

There were those who were not as taken with Ronny and his house calls. But the poor soul had not been given much of a chance in life. Jack Preston reckoned there was a smarter boy in Ronny than most of the villagers suspected, smart enough to curtail his visits to those who did not like him, and perhaps even smart enough to play the fool with everyone else.

30

Now that his presence in the workshop had been discovered, Ronny remained standing and pointed at Jack's bandaged head. After saying "pain" a number of times, Ronny repeated the word "fire". He sounded alarmed at first, as if the blaze had yet to be extinguished, but then his voice took on a grimmer tone. Ronny was angry. Angry with the fire and the pain the fire had inflicted.

Jack Preston calmed the boy, told him he was already feeling much better.

Ronny smiled up at the cobwebs and, seconds later, he seized his chance. It was rare for Jack to pay him this much heed; at best he was allowed to slide behind the wheel of a car Jack was working on and listen to the transistor radio that occupied a permanent spot on a shelf above the workbench, its aerial pointed at the window to pick up the signal from the pirate radio station out to sea. And so Ronny seized his chance and blurted out a dream that consisted of a single word.

"Cortina."

But Jack Preston shook his head. He turned back towards the workbench and once again became absorbed in the curled pages of his order book.

With the exception of Ronny's mother, everyone in Aldstead wound up in the Black Swan at least once a week. The pub's genuine regulars, however, could be counted on the fingers of one hand and every villager could reel off the names of all five.

They would turn up without fail at the same time of day; two sat at the short end of the bar, half hidden by the brick pillar on the corner, the other three took pride of place in front of the beer taps, close to what they liked to call their "barrels of fun". The trio at the taps were younger and more boisterous than Norris and Blunt, who were content with each other's company and the mild wooziness they maintained with the calm steadiness of their drinking, there to be read in the foam that clung to the sides of their glasses as they gazed out of the window at the world they had for a while escaped.

Jack Preston was not in the habit of visiting the Swan on a weekday, but he was unable to wait until Saturday, or even Friday night. He not only wanted to put in an appearance but felt he had to. After all, people knew he was back and they knew full well what had happened; Maureen had told everything when he did not return from France.

But what had they read?

He had arrived home to find two cuttings on the table. One, a newspaper report featuring a not very informative photograph, probably taken when he had already been carried off, stated that both he and Deedee owed their lives to the bodyguard.

Strictly speaking, the bodyguard had not saved anyone.

It was only once the flames had stopped shooting in their direction that the bodyguard had dragged first Deedee, and then Jack, away from the burning Sutton, without any danger to his own life or his extravagantly pomaded and tweaked moustache. He – Jack Preston – had saved Deedee's life. Had he not intervened, the flames would, at the very least, have destroyed her face. And, if the wounds on his back were anything to go by, much more than her face alone.

32

No sooner had Jack Preston closed the door behind him than Norris and Blunt emerged from behind the pillar and greeted him with broad smiles. The doubts that had seized him shortly before he stepped inside evaporated in an instant. Bob the landlord left his island, apron in place and dishcloth in hand, to extend a hearty welcome. Four villagers sitting at a corner table responded in kind to Jack's raised hand and continued to stare at him over their shoulders. People he knew from Sunday morning Mass emerged from the snug and gathered around with Norris and Blunt.

In front of the beer taps sat Rigby, Riley and Vickers, accompanied by Cowe; it was Cowe's bike that Jack had seen leaning against the wall outside, or rather the bike Cowe borrowed from Colin when he did seasonal work up on the farm. It unsettled Jack Preston that this unstable giant of a man barely even looked at him and was the only one not to put his glass down on his beermat as Jack recounted the events on boulevard Albert Premier.

In the silence that followed his concluding words he heard the drip of the tap in the sink behind the bar. Someone in the corner began to clap. With dismissive gestures and a shake of the head, Jack Preston tried to discourage the others from joining in, he had done what anyone else would have done, nothing more, but the applause spread until it filled the Black Swan. The ovation was sincere, no words or cheers or whistles, an expression of respect and admiration.

Cowe let the last of his pint slide slowly into his mouth.

He alone had not applauded. Everyone saw him shrug as he set his glass on the beermat.

They all waited in silence; the man's body language set the tone for his response.

"All I see is bandages."

As the landlord, Bob felt a sense of responsibility and asked Cowe what he meant.

"Bandages," Cowe said deliberately. "That's all I see. Rags wrapped round his head."

"And?"

"What does rags prove? Nothing if you ask me."

Indignant mumbles swelled to declarations of protest.

"Well, what do you lot see?"

That one simple question, from the mouth of a giant at that, left everyone speechless.

"He can say what he likes. I wasn't there. I didn't see him dive on top of Deedee. You?"

A few of those present saw that Jack Preston's hands were feeling for the end of the bandage, and the protest and the indignation flared up once again, more fiercely this time. Cowe was out of line and Jack had nothing to prove.

With almost the same gestures as before, Jack tried to calm the mood. Just as the applause had been unnecessary, now too he saw no harm in repaying their trust – in fact, he insisted on it. At the same time it occurred to him that this spectacle, his show of magnanimity, would soon be the talk of the village.

With pride he remembered that evening two years ago when he had unfolded the letter on the bar, the sheet of paper that bore the green-and-yellow Sutton logo like a royal coat of arms in its letterhead, open to be inspected by those who would not take him at his word.

Face turned to the door, he continued to unwind the bandage and asked for Bob's assistance in rolling it up neatly. He felt the air playing more freely around his head and all of a sudden the dripping tap behind the bar sounded clear as a bell. He was holding the last of the bandage in his hands. Behind him, women sucked a long hiss of breath through gritted teeth, while the tobacco smoke that hung in heavy swathes throughout the Swan at this hour settled around his tender skin like a sheet of sandpaper.

"Burns."

Cowe's tone was unconvinced.

"All I see now is burns."

33

The events of the previous night were repeated: Maureen Coxwold placed her hands on her husband's buttocks. Her initial astonishment at the effect of this simple act had turned to eager expectation.

Halfway through, without stopping, they smiled at each other and were both keenly aware of this bed in this house in Aldstead, under a pale-blue evening sky on the second longest day of the year.

Maureen took the liberty of bringing her hand to her breast and squeezing her nipple between thumb and forefinger, and soon afterwards Jack Preston fell into her with a deep animal cry.

As his weight forced the air from her lungs, it was the sound, that masculine sound, the sweat on his buttocks, the look in his eyes when she had squeezed her nipple, the triumphant culmination of it all that sent her over the brink and into the great wide yonder.

34

Night after night, fire engulfed the dreams of Jack Preston. If he was lucky, his dream had faded by morning and the illusion of having been delivered from it would last the rest of the day.

It was a deafening roar that scorched his flesh: the cells of his body had absorbed the pain and the sound. At night, unchecked, they disgorged their contents. There was no respite. For a brief moment his body fought off the attack, clenched, turned hard as stone, a stone that not only grew hotter but gradually gave in and made concessions to the relentless heat, sacrificing his skin little by little. There was no end to it.

When he woke from the dream, it was not – as one might expect – to find himself sitting bolt upright in bed, bathed in sweat. He lay there next to Maureen, breathing calmly. The transition between sleeping and waking consisted of nothing more than the opening of his eyes. It was as if death were on his heels and, sapped of his last ounce of strength, he had accepted his fate with a liberating equanimity.

Until the thought of Deedee sent his heart racing.

Her face, half-hidden by her blonde hair. Bobbing under the photographers' arms, seeking her freedom, every movement lithe and graceful. Looking at him through the veil of hair, fixing him in her sights even before she straightens up, already laughing at her impulse to take this path to the Prince.

Every step rounded by the supple sway of her hips, joints bathing in the finest oil, a superior motor system.

She laughs at her impulse because she understands what is about to occur. Every step of her path through the crowd has been preordained. She has taken just enough time to stop and talk to the drivers, the press pack has delayed her for exactly the right number of seconds. And now she knows she has to find a gap, slip through under their arms, so that her loping strides will bring her swiftly to Jack Preston.

In whose arms she will be safe.

Her guardian angel.

35

It was pleasant up on the rise. He closed his eyes and inhaled deep draughts of fresh air. Today he felt light, his thoughts were light. The stiff sea breeze that had free rein over the vast expanse of moorland, inhibiting all that grew there, ensured a noticeable difference in temperature with lower-lying Aldstead, tucked out of the wind. Stone was piled on stone as far as the eye could see. Low enclosures that had been here for centuries, that had become part of the landscape.

When the spring and autumn mists rolled in, everyone steered clear of the rise if they could help it. Jack Preston knew why. One morning, when the mist lent proximity to even the smallest of sounds, a motionless shape had appeared no more than ten feet from where he was standing, emerging at an agonisingly slow pace. A sheep. Snow white. The kind of white that does not exist for sheep. He could not remember how long they had looked at each other but, after what seemed like an age, the sheep bowed its head as if to graze. Jack Preston remained frozen to the spot, not daring to move. The fear only took hold when the sheep was swallowed by the mist. One moment it was standing in front of him, the next it had vanished, and when the mist lifted less than a minute later there was no trace of it or any other creature in the wide-open terrain.

The snow-white sheep.

Humidity, the sea air, salt deposits on fleece: it defied every explanation.

The tale of the white sheep was as much a part of the village as the church and the Black Swan.

And then there was the tale of the snow dog.

These were fickle apparitions. They might presage the death of a distant cousin or bring news of a baby on the way. Sometimes no-one died and sometimes a marriage remained childless. The harvest failed, a miner had the narrowest of escapes. It was the Lord who disposed, not a sheep or a dog.

A holiday – *that* was it! Those first days back in Aldstead felt for Jack like being on holiday in his own life, his *old* life. With the prospect of a farewell of one kind or another just around the corner, the certainty of change cast an agreeable glow over everything he knew.

It was an invigorating holiday, impeccably organised. Aldstead shared in his sense of having distinguished himself, and sometimes when he saw one villager or another trudging down the street or recognised a neighbour in the distance by the shabby coat they always wore, he felt pity and forgave everyone who had ever done him harm. Moved by the simplicity of the lives they led on this side of the toll bridge, he pictured a day in the distant future when he would look back on it all, this state of grace, with a nostalgia that was already manifesting itself across the boundaries of time, each morning, in the pit of his stomach.

But that feeling never lasted long.

Soon he was once more able to enjoy that salutary sensation of being on holiday, the blessing of the transitory. In the early evening, when the meal that Maureen had cooked was ready to be served and the day fell definitively into place, this blessing saw him manfully embrace the prospect of that blind bend in the road ahead and, like the most unflinching of racing drivers, he longed to take it at full throttle.

36

Three Grands Prix had been run since Monte Carlo. Stark had won the first of them: Spa-Francorchamps in the sombre forests of the Ardennes, the most beautiful circuit on the calendar.

Jack Preston had heard from no-one. Blackman and Alfie were no doubt hard at work preparing for the team's most important race of the year – the British Grand Prix at Brands Hatch.

Listening to the reports on the radio, Jack Preston was struck by the speed at which the sport was evolving. In Spa-Francorchamps, the commentators were already marvelling at a groundbreaking experiment. He knew Sutton had been developing the technology in secret, but now several teams had wings fitted on the rear of their cars – some on the front too – mounted on struts up to five feet long. An innovation with the potential to change the sport for good. The resistance generated by the resulting airflow pressed down on the wheels, boosting the car's stability and making it capable of faster lap times. They looked ridiculous, but that was the last thing on your mind as you sped across the finish line.

One Grand Prix later he heard that the wings had been banned, at least in their present fragile form. The slender struts buckled under the pressure or their connection to the car's suspension gave way. This always occurred at high speed, when the pressure was at its greatest, a sudden change that sent the car swerving out of control. If the driver was lucky he would hit a pile of straw bales or one of the rare crash barriers, and the fuel tanks on either side of him would remain intact.

From a newspaper photograph taken at Zandvoort, Jack concluded that the Sutton 44 was still racing in its dashing new colours: red, white and gold. And while advertising on the bodywork had become a fact of life, the Navy Cut sailor had given way to the Union Jack. One journalist mused that these rapid changes marked the end of an era that had begun with the garagistas in the late Fifties, a period when everything but the drivers had remained the same, give or take a cylinder or two in the engines. Revenues from advertising and television broadcasts were giving teams the resources to breathe new life into the sport. These were fast-moving times and the world of Formula One was moving with them at last!

37

Standing in front of the tools on the wall, leaning on the edge of his workbench, Jack Preston was among the dunes of Zandvoort or the pines of Francorchamps. Crouching next to the Sutton 44, overalls fresh from the packaging, their sharp creases dividing him into squares. Absorbed in the task at hand, work came first, of course, he glanced up only occasionally. No pats on the shoulder. Everyone knew: no pats on the shoulder. Most of them lightly touched his upper arm, he was hard at work after all. Mechanics, engineers, team bosses, all of the drivers who passed gave a sign of their appreciation, their support, congratulated him, let him know one way or another that they were pleased he was one of them. That he more than deserved the attention bestowed on him. Was that skinflint Blackman paying him enough? Voices above his head, louder than necessary, audible to Blackman on the other side of the car and accompanied by a hammy wink; all laid on so thick that a pay rise might even be on the cards.

<h1 style="text-align:center">38</h1>

The car above the oil pit rocked on its tyres. Ronny had leapt out of the driver's seat and was barking a question. Who was that outside? Jack Preston heard someone call his name. First name and surname, an official occasion, important news. As Ronny stood in the doorway, jiggling with excitement, Jack clambered out of the pit and turned down the radio.

Rigby, who had been dispatched by Bob to relay the message, continued to yell at the top of his voice, wary of setting foot among the looming sheds in the deserted yard without making a racket. That evil mutt was not always chained up, an attack could come from any direction and when he shouted Jack's surname in short, sharp bursts, it had the ring of a malicious snarl that might keep the dog at bay.

Rigby shook Jack by the hand, not something he was accustomed to do.

He had come to convey Bob's decision to put on a bit of a

do to mark the big occasion. Everyone had been invited down to the Black Swan to watch the show. And of course, the evening would hardly be complete without Jack Preston . . .

Hadn't he seen the announcement?

Deedee.

She was due to appear on Edmund Kingsley's chat show this coming Friday. She was starring in a film that was about to start shooting in London. A forty-minute audience with Deedee . . .

On "Kingsley"?

It had escaped his notice even though the doors of the television cabinet in the living room were always open in the evening. He noticed the specks of dandruff in Ronny's parting; the boy stood between the two men, looking from one to the other.

"Kingsley".

Friday.

Deedee.

39

In a daze, Jack Preston worked on one car, then another. He cut his thumb, but he was too bound up in his own thoughts to swear. He even lifted a corner of the tarpaulin from the bonnet of the Cortina. This glimpse alone was enough to send Ronny into raptures. He jumped up and down, and pressed Jack to him, eyes tight shut and a blissful smile on his face. The pain of the embrace was enough to bring Jack to his senses. He sent Ronny home, out of harm's way. Impervious to his anger, the smiling boy set off for the village, arms hanging like dead weights from his shoulders.

In church Jack Preston knelt in the front pew; in the light of recent events, his communication with the Lord had taken a more personal turn.

Immersed in the consecrated peace between these sturdy walls, he reconciled himself with her lengthy silence. How could he have thought that a woman such as Deedee would right the wrongs of Monte Carlo by letter? All this time she had been working on something. Of course she had a plan – he had never doubted her for a moment. Straight after the Grand Prix she had sat down at the table with her entourage, determined to come up with a fitting response. One that reflected the magnitude of his intervention and would be heard by as many people as possible. While the press continued to churn out wide-of-the-mark reports about her bodyguard, Deedee had been waiting for her cue. It had come with Kingsley. Edmund Kingsley and his celebrated shabby sofa.

Jack Preston felt the grace of God.

Saying an Our Father, his bleeding thumb in his mouth, his thoughts strayed to the following week's British Grand Prix.

An invitation from the Automobile Federation was on the cards. Everyone would have watched "Kingsley", and everyone knew that everyone watched "Kingsley".

Who was this man, Jack Preston? The man who had saved Deedee's looks and sent tears rolling down her cheeks live on television? The public had a right to know this man from Aldstead.

On the starting grid and in the stands, his name would be on everyone's lips, spoken in the same breath as Deedee's. The Federation would welcome him with open arms as their guest of honour. Everyone connected with Formula One, near or far, would be delighted to see him again, first shaking his hand before turning their attention to the pompous Federation president who was accompanying him and Deedee on the traditional pre-race walkabout. Never before had a guest of honour been given such a hearty, high-spirited reception from drivers and world champions. Gill, ever the clown, would fall to his knees. And that photograph – Gill kneeling before him with his head bowed like a knight before his king – would make the front pages of the morning papers, a safe bet if ever there was one. The winner of the Grand Prix, unless it was Gill himself, of course, would have to thumb his way through to the sports section, outshone by Gill and Preston and Deedee.

He raised his eyes to Christ on the cross, but he saw a very different image. Deedee was already strolling at his side, slipping her arm through his as they paraded across the starting grid. A spot of lunch before the event. A table draped in starched linen. He was so bold as to fill her glass with water before she could ask. And there, right in front of him, her mouth, those lips, moving smoothly as she chewed.

He shook his head.

But was it so inconceivable?

He took a deep breath that transported him effortlessly back to the beginning. Friday. The Black Swan. Deedee on Kingsley's sofa. Edmund Kingsley, who would waste no time in extending an invitation to Jack Preston, to hear his side of the story. Everyone was curious, and not only about his story. At his host's request he would rise from the sofa and turn his back to the studio audience, the cameras and the watching world. Kingsley would be ready to spring into action, only too eager to help. Awkward titters at first, as he fumbled with the bandage, then silence. The heat of the studio lights, tilted to focus on the tender scars, a distant memory of the fire.

In the shadow of one of the cypresses he lit a cigarette and smoked as if his life depended on it. It sent his head spinning.

He had to stay calm.

The Lord was with him.

At home, Maureen did not seem surprised by the news, as if she had known for days. He pondered this and then dismissed it. She set the table and smiled sweetly, brought him a glass of beer. "My hero," she whispered.

Under the thin, white fabric of her blouse he caught a faint suggestion of something darker. Was he seeing straight? Was she really not wearing a bra?

She held his thumb like a nestling in her palm.

With the greatest of care, she turned it towards the light.

She examined the cut.

Her eyes misted over with a quiet contentment.

40

The next day, Maureen brought him an apple, a banana and the post.

Early that morning she had cycled to the market in Little Habton, her head floating just above the mist that veiled the landscape. The prospect of another summer's day glowed pink and purple on the horizon. All the way she was filled with a jubilation that she was barely able to contain. It bubbled over spontaneously into fleeting prayers; like her husband she believed in balance, in a Lord who giveth and taketh away.

Maureen was aware of her body as she cycled: her movements were those of a woman, she felt this in her back and neck, in her shoulders and her hips, the way in which the force sank through her tensed calves and pointed feet and into the pedals, so casually that it seemed as if the bicycle was moving her legs.

Where the road curved towards the coast, she heard the squabbling of the gulls over the dunes and felt the calm immensity of the sleeping water as an immeasurable part of her own happiness.

41

With one hand resting on her handlebars and a paper bag in the other, she stood in the open doorway, the sun beating down on her back, her contours divulged. She said she had brought the post. The post, an apple and a banana.

She knew her husband did not appreciate her dropping

in at his workshop. She said she had run into her brother at the market in Little Habton. News of Deedee's appearance on "Kingsley" was spreading like wildfire there too. He would be coming over to the Black Swan on Friday to watch, with a few of the lads from work.

"Post?"

"Yes, a letter."

She leaned her bicycle against the shed, removed the envelope from the paper bag and held out her arm without moving from the spot.

She always felt as if she were embarrassing him some-how, although there was no-one else around and he had assured her many times that this was not the case. He had plenty of work to do, but never so much that he was unable to put down his tools for five minutes. What about when he smoked a cigarette? Did he carry on working then? These were questions and comments she had long since learned to keep to herself, knowing Jack would react as if he had been stung by a wasp. Now she paid him a visit only if a letter arrived for him, and even that did not always go down well.

He walked over to her, took the letter and thanked her for the fruit. He allowed her to take a step closer and with an audible sigh she pressed the tip of her nose against his cheek.

"For you," she said quietly. "Don't go giving them to Ronny."

After he had waved the paper bag in the air by way of farewell and she had disappeared around the corner, he looked at the envelope. It was upside down, but he recognised the red, white and gold of the new logo.

Gold Leaf Team Sutton.

The colours. The name. He wondered if he would ever get used to them.

42

The letter was signed by someone he did not know, on behalf of Blackman. It was a long letter, three hefty paragraphs. He stepped outside and sat on the front wheel of the weed-choked tractor to read it. Dear Mr Preston. When he had finished, he stared out over the cornfield for a while. He took the pack of cigarettes from his breast pocket and lit up. When he had finished smoking, he read the letter a second time.

He had been sacked.

Not that it was there in black and white. On a page full of words, the word dismissal did not appear.

The epistle was an exercise in self-pity. The company

was at the mercy of multiple forces, primarily commercial. If it was to survive in these times of ruthless competition and continue to focus on the passion that had sparked it all – the love of motor racing – the company had no choice. Image was everything. In the wake of recent developments – which could only mean the blaze in Monte Carlo – the team had been subject to the wrong kind of scrutiny. An intervention was needed to restore the balance, to ensure that Gold Leaf Team Sutton would once again be synonymous with technical ingenuity and youthful sporting prowess.

Jack Preston read this last sentence over and over again.

The blame for the fire was being laid at his door. He was a scapegoat being sent into the wilderness. He was too old. At the age of thirty-five, brilliantine in his hair, he was too old for this "youthful" team. Too old for a brand of cigarettes that young people were smoking.

Whatever the reason, he had been sacked.

He smoked another cigarette and ate the banana.

Time passed, and he began to shake his head and smile. They had missed the announcement. They did not know that Deedee was appearing on "Kingsley". This Friday. Someone at Gold Leaf Team Sutton would soon be tearing his hair out, would be facing dismissal himself. Image was everything, after all.

A new letter would be on its way, and soon, dispatched by courier in the hope that it would arrive before the British Grand Prix, beating the rival teams to the punch. By then they would all have got wind of his dismissal. That letter would contain no reference to this one. It would announce a rise in remuneration due to his "recent efforts". Along with the drivers, he would become the face of the team, an example to young people everywhere.

43

That night he dreamed of Enzo Ferrari.

At first he saw only his face, stern as ever. Through the blue-tinted lenses in their striking black frames, the Italian looked him straight in the eye and spoke these words:

A man who goes through fire for beauty belongs with Ferrari.

Arm outstretched, he placed his hand on Jack Preston's shoulder, looking around to make sure everyone was taking note of this gesture.

There had been no pain.

At the breakfast table he took the proposal under consideration.

He would have to live abroad temporarily, close to the

headquarters in Maranello. Several months of the year at least.

Perhaps he could negotiate a modest house on the French Riviera, just over the Italian border, a stone's throw from Monaco, within striking distance of Nice. A stone-built house, no carpets, ochre walls. Cicadas and lizards.

Did Ferrari mechanics drive a Ferrari?

Possibly not, but wouldn't he be an exception, having been brought into the fold by Signor Enzo himself?

Deedee and her friends would make the necessary introductions and before long his own Mediterranean lifestyle would take shape, populated by important and even famous figures, people who nevertheless did not spend all their time in the spotlight. They would meet at Monte Carlo's finest restaurants and frequent the casino; ever mindful of his own humble beginnings, he would be sure to have a private word with the man who parked his Ferrari. Each member of his circle possessed a singular talent or merit and it was this that united them, in all their diversity, to lead a life of privilege. It was privilege they wore lightly, determined not to let it spoil their fun. Having mastered the art of living, they shared their wisdom generously.

Arriving at the door to his workshop, he woke from his reverie but only briefly, for once inside he took up position in front of the map nailed to the wall next to his work-bench. He stared into the faded blue of the Mediterranean and then turned his attention to the principality itself, to its streets. Those that formed part of the circuit were drawn wider than the rest, allowing ample space for the capitals that spelled their names.

Boulevard Albert Premier.

Avenue d'Ostende.

One by one he whispered them, rolling them around his mouth, tasting with rapture the world that awaited him.

44

When it was all over, Jack Preston wished he had watched the programme at home in his living room, without the distraction of the eyes that had been turned in his direction. At home he would have been able to study her face closely, to gauge her expression as she spoke certain words.

The evening began in the morning, as soon as he opened his eyes. All day he tinkered with an engine while his mind was in the Black Swan, in a hotel room at an undisclosed location and, as the day wore on, at a television studio in London. Having scrubbed the dirt from his pores and put on his best suit in front of the bedroom mirror, he decided the time had come to dispense with his bandages. From now on his head would remain uncovered and he would wear his scars like a veteran wears his military honours. He held up his wife's hand mirror behind him and saw a hairline that ran from ear to ear across the crown of his head. Only the top of his right ear had a shrivelled ridge of cartilage. Face on, no-one could suspect the havoc wrought on his skull and the nape of his neck.

Maureen told him to sit on a kitchen chair and tucked a clean tea towel into his collar. Her fingertips barely touched the scars, a relief of once-molten skin. He felt nothing as she trimmed his hair, pressing her warm body against him. On the way to the Black Swan she was in high spirits. She linked her arm through his and the weight of her hips danced as she stepped lightly. When he searched for his lighter she slid her hand deep into his trouser pocket and feigned surprise at what she found there.

Their entrance was like a stone plunging into water: ripples spread audibly towards the edges of the packed pub. Rigby, Riley and Vickers were lost in the crowd, but Cowe's grinning mug over by the beer taps stuck out head and shoulders above everyone else. Bob waved from the raised island where he and his daughter were busy pulling pints. He must have instructed people to make way for them, as the crowd parted instantly to leave a path through the middle of the Swan. The few chairs were already taken, among their occupants Norris and Blunt who had abandoned their regular barstools in favour of a prime spot in front of the telly. A few minutes later, Jack and Maureen both had a glass in their hand – he a pint, she a gin and orange – and when at last the familiar theme tune began, the opening credits rolled and the people down the front hissed for quiet, he felt Ronny worm his way between them, without so much as a word or a glance.

45

Kingsley stood in front of his desk, welcomed everyone to the show and told a couple of jokes that were lapped up by the studio audience but failed to raise a chuckle in the Swan. Then, turning on the rakish charm, he announced his special guest, his only guest of the evening, a remarkable young woman with whom everyone wanted to become better acquainted, he being no exception – wink, wink. And so, without further ado, this evening, ladies and gentlemen, it was his great pleasure to introduce – he made a grand gesture towards the side of the stage – Deedee!

Jack Preston's heart pounded as if he had been waiting

in the wings for his own name to be called. Hesitant applause broke out behind him, a wolf whistle came from the direction of the bar: none of this made any impact as, for the first time since Monte Carlo, he saw her again. Deedee. He watched her walk on set, emerging from behind a panel where she must have been standing as Kingsley cracked his corny jokes, Deedee again, at last, live on television, those long, leisurely strides of hers, the enchanting way she placed her foot directly in front of her slender figure, casual and unfaltering, a cat sauntering along the top of a fence.

As applause continued to fill the studio, a wordless exchange took place beside the shabby sofa, a trading of looks and gestures, do I really have to sit on this, yes, I'm sorry, tradition dictates, at which she, with a deadpan expression and much to Kingsley's amusement, proceeded to brush off the seat cushion and balance her behind on its very edge. The camera zoomed in and Deedee's face all but filled the curved surface of the television screen in the Black Swan.

46

Her make-up was heavier, he noticed, her clear blue eyes rimmed with a darker shadow. In Monaco her frivolity had seemed to be a product of her tender years, but today she struck him as being a woman. On the brink, not quite there. A grown-up girl on the verge of womanhood, aching for the transition to occur. She was desire personified, while an innocence and candour still clung to her, disarming everyone. Unlike the Hollywood stars of old she had not descended from on high, but had come from an ordinary village where until recently she had gone to school and attended Holy Mass. Her innocence had been tempered by the world's attentions, which reached her by way of Telstar's bleeping orbit and were concentrated in the camera's lens. Her every gesture spoke of life itself, rehearsal and completion in one – a scintillating riddle.

47

In the first ten minutes, the surface babble of conversation was disturbed only sporadically by a white-crested wave – an insinuation by the host, a giggle from Deedee, a burst of appreciative applause, followed by the rearrangement of hairstyles and seating positions. The greatest excitement lay in the simple fact of her physical presence on Kingsley's sofa and her accent, which gave every word that passed her lips a suggestive charge.

Just as the thoughts of the Black Swan's punters were returning to beer and the general murmur rose above the steady drip of the tap behind the bar, Kingsley inserted a dramatic pause. With the hint of a lopsided smile, he stared out from under his brows into countless living rooms. After what felt to Jack Preston like an eternity, the host explained that while Deedee had, of course, accepted his invitation to talk about her new film, as we had all just heard, she also – he weighed his words carefully – had a special announcement to make. After another pause his eyebrows shot up and he fixed Deedee with a penetrating stare.

Out of the corner of his eye, Jack Preston saw heads turn in his direction, felt eyes on his back and the nape of his neck . . .

As if startled by her host's manner, Deedee clasped her hands to the pendant that dangled just below her throat. She told the world that she was to be the new sidekick to John Steed in the popular television series "The Avengers". "You?" Kingsley stammered. "You're to be our new Emma Peel?" She nodded quickly, excited as a child. Cheering and clapping erupted in the studio. Kingsley sat open-mouthed a tad too long for his surprise to be genuine and the hilarity he was intending to trigger eventually won out over the applause. He asked Deedee whether she had seen "The Avengers", if she was aware of the kind of catsuits Emma Peel wore in her fight against crime? Another bout of enthusiastic nodding ensued and Deedee revealed that she already wore them at home sometimes. She lowered her eyes and brushed her hand across her miniskirt as if trying to make it longer.

48

With dawn in sight Jack Preston gave up; sleep was not going to come. He rolled over and lay on his back, something he was able to keep up for longer each time. The scar tissue was growing harder, gradually offering more protection than pain.

I love you.

She had put the emphasis on "you". Perhaps this had been deliberate. Perhaps it had nothing to do with her accent. I love *you*. And then she had put her hand to her lips and blown a kiss in close-up.

She had not said "I love you all".

Before they went off air – the band had already struck up the tune that ended the show – Kingsley asked hurriedly if she had a message for the British viewers, so hurriedly that it appeared unrehearsed. It seemed to Jack that they had genuinely lost track of time. For the first time in forty minutes Deedee looked straight into the camera, without hesitation, as if she had been ready for this moment. Her voice was all of a sudden deeper, more intimate. She sounded and looked as if she were thinking only of one person, her message intended for him alone.

She did not say "I love you all" . . .

They had lost track of time.

At the very last moment Kingsley had given her the opportunity to address herself to him, to Jack Preston. She had come straight to the point, realising there was no time to mention his name. He deserved better. She could not simply mention his name without any introduction, without paying tribute to what he had done.

I love *you*.

Not a word had been spoken about the fire in the course of the interview. There were no questions about Monte Carlo. Was the subject taboo? Had Sutton insisted? Or had Kingsley consigned it to the past, too long ago to merit a mention? Besides, Deedee had emerged unscathed. It was water under the bridge, no longer newsworthy. But a brief message to Jack Preston, that was still possible, in the dying seconds of the programme.

Just as they ran out of time.

The villagers at the Swan must have understood this too. He had been the focus of their applause after all. Someone had shaken him firmly by the hand and before he knew it almost everyone in the place had come up to congratulate him. There seemed to be no doubt in their minds who Deedee's parting kiss had been intended for.

Jack Preston willingly accepted their compliments but could not shake the thought that the reaction at the Swan might merely be attributed to expectations. It stayed with him in spite of the beer and stared up at him from the bottom of every glass. The whole idea had been to make a festive evening of it, a party in his honour. Perhaps the enthusiasm after the show had simply been relief that at least one thing said on "Kingsley" might have been intended for the man of the evening, a last-minute validation of the festivities.

On the way home, he could still feel handshake after handshake and hear laughter echoing close to his ear. A skyful of stars twinkled high above Aldstead, the same stars, he thought, that shone over London and Deedee. Maureen assured him that the fleeting, anonymous gesture of gratitude was only a beginning. That he would soon be back at work. In sight of the church, which stood like a sentinel holding back the darkness at the edge of the village, Maureen answered his unasked question:

"Of course Deedee loves you . . . We all love you."

49

No letter of rectification came from Gold Leaf Team Sutton. Jack Preston was not invited to attend the British Grand Prix. At the hour the race was held he stood in front of his workshop staring out across the cornfield. He smoked slowly, lost in thought. On Sunday, this far from the village, it was so quiet that high in the sky he could make out the faint, familiar sound of a swarm of racing cars, although strictly speaking that was impossible.

50

On Monday, shortly after midday, he walked into the cornfield.

Something came over him. He observed himself taking a long, last draw on his cigarette, flicking the fag end away between thumb and middle finger and setting off towards the corn. Colin and his farmhands had left at the crack of dawn to work on the ploughed land over by the medieval bridge, Cowe perched on the mudguard of one of the tractors. Jack Preston ate a banana, then lit a cigarette, and as he stared at the view that had been etched on his mind for years, the decision welled up inside him.

Even as he took the first steps he found it inexplicable that he had never done this before; the field had always been there, open to all. It was not as far as he thought it would be. He halted at the edge of the vast, deep-yellow sea. The wind washed in rustling waves over the ripe ears of corn. Billy had perked up from a doze and was standing staunchly, tail sweeping broadly to and fro.

Nor was the corn as tall as it appeared from his workshop. Halfway across the field he came to a stop, it dizzied him just as gazing up from the foot of an office block can make a person dizzy. He smiled. This too was an observation.

He turned and looked back at the farmyard, deep in his field of vision. Billy barked once and reared up half-heartedly. It was as if the dog wanted to jump up at him despite the distance. He surveyed the farm and its surroundings. The green glimmer of moss on the far sheds, where only the evening sun penetrated, seemed to him like a creeping effort to lay waste to this misguided huddle of man-made structures.

Before long his eyes were drawn to a dark place, the open doors of his workshop. The entrance to his life. Ronny came shambling up, arms hanging at his sides, pale face tilted upwards, neat parting in his black hair. Jack Preston stood still as a tree in a meadow. He saw the boy disappear inside and wander out a little later, with exactly the same shambling gait. It was Monday, shortly after midday. He stood in the middle of his familiar view looking the other way and made another decision.

51

The Cortina was not a Cortina. Not really. The car of Ronny's dreams, the car under the tarpaulin, was a Sutton Cortina: a special, sporting model that had shrugged off almost every resemblance to the popular Ford family saloon on which it was based. In 1963, Blackman himself had conjured the power of 105 stampeding horses – or, better still, bull terriers straining at the leash – from a 1500 c.c. four-cylinder twin-cam engine. Its extra-long first and second gear enabled the Sutton Cortina to make a raw, husky transition from a standing start to sixty in ten seconds flat. To keep its weight to a minimum, the doors and the bonnet were made of aluminium, but relatively heavy steering ensured that she was anything but a biscuit tin on wheels; the Sutton Cortina was a street fighter and the driver needed both hands to keep her under control.

Jack Preston whipped off the tarpaulin in a single motion.

Standing next to the car, he once again found himself lost in admiration. Clean lines and character in one. He loved her angles, her low suspension. Her colours were those of a true Sutton: white bodywork and a broadening band of green starting with a pinpoint at the headlights and sweeping back along her sides to the modest dorsal fins that flanked the boot to create the illusion of speed. Round headlights. Round tail lights, divided into three equal segments, mirroring the design of the dashboard ventilator. The green-and-yellow Sutton emblem on the front grille, and printed along the narrow edge of a stream-lined ridge on the bonnet, the word "Cortina".

How, Jack Preston wondered, could anyone ever improve on this?

Sutton had cut him loose, but that could not shake his love for this car, offered to him at a knockdown price two years earlier, not long after joining the team. He took the ignition key from the hook beside the transistor radio and slid into the bucket seat; no pain yet. The car started immediately, hungrily, with a snarl born of waiting too long.

On the few occasions that Jack Preston had taken the Cortina for a spin, he had pushed her hard. The car demanded it; Blackman had built her with that purpose in mind. In a long loop he headed for the toll bridge, to blow the dust out of her engine on the roads he knew best. Roads used only by farmers, some stretches lined by high verges and wooded banks that closed in on him like a tunnel.

Not long now until the trees. He felt the excitement build, a tingling on the back of his head. The trees were old, bare-branched and crooked, choked by thick tangles of unruly green. Trees from a dark, prehistoric time, each long branch ending in a tiny tree of dried twigs – a clutch of fossilised claws. They stood scattered on either side of a sloping section of road.

He took a deep breath as he came out of the bend, shifted into third gear, put his foot down. Passing the gate to the meadow, within sight of the trees, he closed his eyes and let go of the wheel. Calmly he began to count, up to six as always. Eyes closed and hands flat on his thighs, he pressed his foot down and counted to six. The Cortina's high revs filled his ears and God illuminated the darkness. As before, He took control of the wheel and kept Jack safe from harm, steering him through the deadly trees.

52

At the toll bridge he had a moment's hesitation, but once he was clear of the rattling beams he set a determined course for London. The revving of the Cortina, the throb of her engine, released a deep sense of joy within him. He had taken the right decision.

Two hours later, Jack Preston did not even have to negotiate the city centre; the neighbourhood in which Deedee was shooting the film, the one she had talked about on "Kingsley", was on the near side of the capital. "That way," a newsagent said, pointing wearily at one of the walls of his shop without looking up. "Three minutes."

A dog track.

A gaggle of teenage girls had gathered outside the gates, elated and impatient. Had it not been the holidays, they might have been waiting for a bus to come and whisk them off on a school trip. He edged his way through the crowd, which was fringed by clusters of young men, lanky characters with unkempt hair. Detached from the excitement, they remained at a close remove, eyeing the girls like vultures.

The larger of the two guards, a man Jack's own age, looked at the friendly hand extended towards him with an air of mild surprise. As they shook hands, Jack Preston introduced himself. Once he had said his name a second time, the guard seemed to understand and disappeared without a word into the cabin behind him.

He returned with a sheet of paper.

"What was the name again?"

"Jack Preston."

The guard ran his finger down the list.

Jack helpfully repeated his name, leaving a pause between first name and surname. The guard asked him if he knew about the times. The delivery times. Jack Preston apologised for the misunderstanding. He had not come to deliver anything. He had come to see Deedee.

"To see Deedee?"

"Yes. Didn't she let you know?"

"Your name isn't on the list."

"But perhaps she told you she was expecting me?"

"No," the guard said. "If she had, your name would be on the list."

Standing shoulder to shoulder, both men looked from

the sheet of paper to the teenagers in the car park.

"I was there in Monte Carlo. When the fire broke out. I'm a mechanic with Team Sutton . . ."

The guard took a good long look at Jack Preston's disfigured head.

"I'm sure she'll be only too happy to see me if she knows I'm here."

"Are you Jerry Stark's mechanic?"

"Yes, that's me. Jack Preston . . ."

"Why aren't you on the list?"

"Because we didn't make an appointment. That's all."

The guard withdrew into his own thoughts.

The second he opened the small gate in the railings, the girls let out a piercing howl. The guard marched up to the nearest building and disappeared inside. The door slammed shut behind him. Five minutes later another door opened, triggering an outburst of girlish hysteria. At first, no-one came out.

53

As if the screaming had pierced his eardrums and he was oblivious to the commotion in the car park, the guard coolly made his way back to his post.

"My boss says you could be the pope for all he cares. Your name's not on the list."

His demeanour turned steely. As far as he was concerned, that was the end of the matter.

Jack Preston thanked him.

"You did all you could."

A little surprised once again, the guard shook the hand held out to him.

Jack Preston spent the whole day in the car park at the dog track. In the company of the assembled youngsters, he seemed like a passer-by, an ill-informed local who had made a brief detour to see what all the fuss was about before continuing on his way. He was conspicuous and invisible at the same time. Not one of the girls spoke to him.

The next day, Maureen packed him a lunch.

The guard recognised him and relaxed his stern expression for a moment by way of greeting. Jack Preston waited a while before handing him the note he had written the previous evening.

"I'm not allowed to accept letters or gifts for Deedee."

Was it a coincidence that the guard glanced at his young colleague? Or was it a sign?

Jack Preston positioned himself unobtrusively between

the two and tried again. The note disappeared into the guard's large hand and then behind his back as he said in a loud voice, "Sorry. No letters. I won't tell you again."

54

What happened to the note would remain a mystery.

On the third day, two different men were guarding the gate. Jack Preston walked up and said hello, but they stared straight ahead impassively, as if he did not exist.

He stepped into one guard's line of vision.

"Jack Preston. Deedee is expecting me."

The man looked him stoically in the face.

"You have to let me in. Check the list."

He told them Deedee was expecting him, that he was the man who had saved her face from the flames in Monte Carlo. That without him there would be no film. He said he was on the list.

He turned and presented the back of his head to the guard.

"See? Take a good look. I have to see her."

Facing the guard again, he leaned closer and said, "I have the *right* to see her."

The two men grabbed Jack Preston by the collar and

frogmarched him through the crowd of horrified girls to the side of the road.

They warned him. They ordered him to leave Deedee alone.

They told him he should be ashamed of himself.

55

That evening the gate to the dog track opened.

The railings rolled slowly to one side on squeaking wheels. Rain had been falling steadily since noon and had washed the car park clean. Jack Preston stood alone at the side of the road, his patience rewarded at last.

It was late, almost dark. The glare of headlights blinded him as a line of cars passed through the gate, four in all. The first stopped beside him, waiting for a chance to turn onto the road; two men in front, the passenger was smoking. Then the miniature caravan began to move; the second and third cars followed in quick succession. Bringing up the rear was a sportscar, a red M.G. with a black folding top.

He recognised her at once, her profile, her hair. Hands high on the wheel, back straight, the bearing of a young driver who was still unsure of herself. He stood in her line of sight, on the side of the oncoming traffic. Here she was, about to stop, get out, invite him to join her in the M.G., exactly as he had imagined. It was filthy weather and he approached the car to save her getting wet.

Here she was, waiting for him.

Deedee.

56

All the way to Aldstead, the question kept running through his mind. Why had he not turned around? Deedee did not know his face. His face had been a blur, a shadow she had looked beyond to where the Prince stood waiting on the steps – if any sight could have sparked recognition in her, it would have been the back of his head.

He could now rule out the possibility that she had received his note. Nevertheless, Jack Preston left home the following morning in high spirits. Deedee too must have given the incident some thought. Perhaps it had dawned on her who he was, the man in the rain who had circled her car, opened the door and almost climbed in.

When he reached the trees he counted to six and kept his eyes shut one beat longer. Seven.

At the toll bridge he barely eased up on the accelerator.

The car park at the dog track was deserted.

No teenage girls, no guards, no-one. He looked around. Someone was playing a joke on him.

The small gate in the railings was not locked. He stepped inside as if it had always been his to pass through, as if he had only temporarily been denied access.

From the stands he looked out over the track, searching for traces of what had taken place here, screened off from the outside world. He searched for traces of her, though he had no idea what form they might take. Deedee had been here, that much was certain. This place had been stirred and altered by her presence.

In the empty stands, looking down on the deserted dog track, he was once again alone with her, entwined in their embrace. A grandstand full of people at boulevard Albert Premier bear witness. She breaks free of the suffocating circle of people of which she is always the centre. She bobs under arms, laughing freely now, looking at him, past him. It all moves quickly, one fluid motion, pulsing to the sway of her hips. She is at the back wheel of the Sutton 44 and at close range, a few feet away, then closer still, he looks upon the radiant face of a perfect being, framed in gold. He looks into that face and sees God's work. It nails him to the ground and at that moment he is blown away by an invisible cloud. They embrace as if no other outcome is possible, as if they both already knew, were waiting for the first drop of fuel to hit the red-hot bodywork. He protects her, his cheek pressed to hers. He covers her, a human shield for what must be saved at any price. In those few seconds time slows to a stop and they are one. One scream. One life.

57

In the weeks that followed, Jack Preston did not miss a single broadcast of "Kingsley". He could not help it. At the beginning or the end of the show, or perhaps between guests, Kingsley would set the record straight. Even without her presence on the sofa, Deedee's wish would be granted: her thanks would be relayed to the English mechanic.

That was why the newspapers maintained their silence. That was why Deedee let nothing slip to the magazines that Maureen perused weekly. Through Kingsley she could reach half the country at a single stroke.

If one of those magazines lay open on the table as he passed on his way to the kitchen or the toilet, pictures of Deedee would sometimes catch his eye. He saw her surrounded by forced smiles and flushed cheeks, grinning mugs in sharp contrast to her modest beauty. Parvenus, the lot of them; parasites who fed off her fame and who were not worthy to appear in the same photograph as her.

On September 18, it was a Saturday, he recognised a man in one of those photographs. In the background, turned from the camera, was the bodyguard who had dragged them both away from the burning Sutton. The moustache. He still had that extravagant moustache, tweaked at the ends.

Beneath the photograph, his name was mentioned.

Why?

Why would they mention the name of her bodyguard?

Jack Preston slammed up the toilet lid with such force that it broke into five pieces.

58

The chill of autumn arrived unannounced; startled summer retreated into the church where it clung on for less than a week between walls as thick as an arm is long. Every morning Ronny gathered wood for the stove in the workshop, a handful of wet, mossy twigs rooted from the soil over by the far sheds, and Jack Preston played along as he had done for years, maintaining the illusion that they were both nice and cosy thanks to the boy's efforts.

There were times when Jack found himself becoming lost in his work. A stubborn bolt could absorb his thoughts and actions until he became every inch the muscular mechanic, his only objective to separate one piece of metal from another.

When Ronny was not droning along to the music on the radio, he was imitating the sound of a racing car rapidly changing gear. His hands would glide over the steering wheel of a car or a delivery van as he leaned into tight bends on either side until he almost rocked himself out of the driver's seat. Actually turning the steering wheel was forbidden. When Jack emerged from the oil pit, the boy would point at his head in undiluted awe and begin to hiss. Then it was a matter of waiting for the rest of the word. "Ss-ss-ss . . ." Ronny poured all his energy into what came next, veins bunched in his temples: the breath and the effort and the word – everything piled up against the barrier of his impediment and his admiration. "Ss-ss-scars."

Jack Preston took a secret pleasure in disappearing back into the oil pit before the poor boy could get his word out. The urge was stronger than he was.

59

One afternoon, after they had shared Jack's lunch and he had let the boy take the last few puffs on his cigarette, Ronny came out with a story about Cowe. His halting words were angry, indignant. It wasn't just Cowe. Even villagers who treated Ronny as one of the family had spoken of his hero in a way that bothered him and made him even angrier as he recalled their words; spit frothed at the corners of his mouth.

Jack Preston had noticed a change himself. On Sunday after Mass, only Jakes and Carlisle, two farmers old as the hills, came up to him and shook his hand in the shadow of the church, churning out the sighs and mutterings that passed as their standard conversation. The other parishioners seemed to be avoiding him.

He sent Ronny away.

He wanted to be alone with his thoughts.

Earlier than usual he dragged the left door along the rail, followed by the right. With a heightened awareness of his own actions, he turned the key in the old padlock. No, he told himself, no need to turn around. I know there's no-one standing in the bare field – no farmhands, no-one from the village. He refused to let his gaze wander across the hillside, but even so, he felt as if eyes were trained on him.

White sheep or snow dog, it was the Lord who disposed.

He wiped his feet by the porch, dipped his fingertips in the holy water and made a sign of the cross. Kneeling in the front pew, he clasped his hands like a communicant.

It was all because he had been sacked.

The scepticism stirred up by Cowe had spread like an oil slick and the fact of his dismissal had undermined the truth. Sutton's decision to sack him had everything to do with the tall tales he had spread about his injuries. That was what people thought.

His own thoughts drifted back to that evening at the Black Swan. Those handshakes after the interview with Deedee, had that been pity? Even then?

The laughter. Had they been mocking him?

60

At the end of October, Jack Preston bought a colour television, the first in Aldstead and Little Habton. "The Avengers", co-starring Deedee, was to be the first programme filmed and broadcast in colour.

The television was of a modern design with slender legs. Two sturdy delivery men, one with letters tattooed on his fingers, the other with rings through his ears, carried the lightweight set into the cottage with embarrassed ease, abandoning it on the spot where its predecessor had left its imprint on the carpet.

Although the television was too expensive and the order book in the workshop had become harder to fill, Maureen did not complain. By some small miracle Jack had been able to buy the set on hire purchase. She would save the monthly instalment by cutting down on their household expenses or taking in a little extra sewing; it was what her husband wanted and she wanted what he wanted, for she wanted *him*, Jack, more than ever. She wanted him every second of the day, a desire so overwhelming that the longing for a child had vanished without trace from her body.

The place where the scar tissue seemed to seethe its way up from the sharp collar of his blue shirt to the back of his head was irresistible to her fingertips. It was the place where her husband revealed himself as a warrior, his naked armour. Even thinking about that touch was enough to trigger dreadful surges of lust from which she would wake in amazement on the kitchen floor or in a cold bath, often with a household implement between her legs as a mute and incongruous witness to what had occurred. Reconstructing the episode little by little, she would sit in front of the bedroom mirror and, looking at herself as if she were another woman, experience her lust anew. With a combination of guilt and marital devotion, her only desire then was to surrender that evening to the power of his loins, his animal cry, a desire that taunted her for the rest of the afternoon, not to be driven out by any domestic chore and to which, lying on his side of the bed, she would eventually succumb, swiftly and intemperately.

61

The quieter and more distant Jack Preston became in the evenings, the more Maureen longed for him.

Once the television had been switched on, he would not tolerate a single word being spoken. From the beginning to the end of the evening's programming, there was no tearing him away from the set.

He searched for an explanation and found none. He saw Deedee appearing on screen in an endless parade of miniskirts and catsuits, seductively coiffed and made up: every day, every morning at the studio, he thought, she sits in front of a mirror and looks at that face - how can she not think of me? If every mirror reminded her of Monte Carlo, of the horror she had escaped, how could she not think him worthy of a sign of gratitude? Did she ever think of him, somewhere in a village in England, the man who *had* been disfigured by the flames?

Only a few months earlier he had been seized by the fleeting, restless urge to embrace the new and uncharted vistas life had in store. Now, day after day, he was swamped by dismay at being deprived of something that he alone deserved.

The Lord would restore the balance.

Surely he was not asking too much? One sign, that was all. One unequivocal sign.

Thinking out loud or praying to God. The difference between the two was no longer clear.

62

On a Friday afternoon, as he stood having a quick cigarette by one of the cypresses before going into the church, he heard the clack of high heels on the path below. It was Bob's daughter, from the Swan. She ploughed along the pavement as if determined not to slacken her pace until she was home and dry on the other side of the village.

Her skirt was so skimpy that it barely covered her backside. With no hope of buying a skirt like it anywhere but the city, she had torn the pattern from a magazine and, unbeknown to Jack, had got Maureen to run it up for her. Her pale thighs above the black knee-length boots made her look more naked than if she had been walking down the street wearing nothing at all – greyish skin pocked with pink blooms from the biting cold.

In his time, Jack Preston had seen plenty of women who dressed like Deedee. The streets of London and Monaco were full of them. But the sight of Bob's daughter on the worn flagstones of Aldstead, clacking past the church where he had attended her first Holy Communion and her confirmation, struck him as an invasion. At the very least it seemed to herald the advance of forces camped on the other side of the toll bridge. The world was snapping at his heels and before long he would be trampled mercilessly underfoot.

He watched Bob's daughter until she disappeared from view. He pictured his wife as he first knew her more than ten years earlier, so very young. Maureen Coxwold. It had been a different world, a time when young women had wanted to look older, worldly-wise and sophisticated, with deep red lips and a pointed bosom. Today women decked themselves out as little girls, parading around on long naked legs.

But the woman on whom they modelled themselves was transcendent. Even the banality of the colour broadcasts that ruthlessly exposed the paint-by-numbers mediocrity of many a co-star could not touch Deedee. It was everything about her, not least the way she moved. Her eyes and her lips especially. There was no need for her to speak. She had already said it all.

63

Staring himself blind through the old windowpane at the other-worldly white of the landscape, his workshop only accessible to farm vehicles and Land Rovers, Jack Preston kept returning to that moment on boulevard Albert Premier.

The nasty taste of the tape he used to cover up the sailor's head fills his mouth. The heavy heat of an unseasonably warm spring day in Monte Carlo settles on his skin. The sensation of eyes watching him from the stands. He feels his heart begin to race as Deedee breaks with protocol, seems to look at him, comes his way. For the first time since the fire he sees the strand of blonde hair that sticks to her moist skin, curving from behind her ear to the hollow at the base of her throat, the full length of her neck exposed by the speed at which she acts upon her impulse. She is so close. But he cannot smell her. No, what he smells is the fuel, changing form, unfurling rapidly in a cloud of heat that surges against his back and envelops him, and then he stops time in its tracks.

This is the moment when he moves his arm.

He reaches out to Deedee, but why?

Can he rule out the possibility that it is a simple act of self-preservation? A reflex? The instinctive urge to reach for something to hold on to as he is blown off his feet? Can he honestly say he is thinking of *her* safety when he stretches out his arm and lands on top of her . . . ?

Does it matter?

He embraces her after all. He understands the heat. He presses her to the ground and broadens his back as the fire gnaws into him.

64

He was a car mechanic. The words emerged from the darkness and hung between the beams above the bed. He tinkered with engines, a fact every driver, every customer took for granted. The most ordinary thing in the world. He would never be an engineer. Never head up a team. Never. There were a great many things he would never be while always remaining Jack Preston, car mechanic. Of Aldstead. Over the toll bridge, in the shadow of the rise, in a shed on Colin's farm. No cicadas, no salamanders sunbathing on a whitewashed wall. He had no golden ticket. He had the key to a padlock and a chained-up dog to greet him. A pew at the front of the church where he knelt to remember his parents. He had a loving wife with slender shoulders and pale eyes, and so it would remain. He felt ashamed. He had let himself get carried away. Ferrari would never know who he was. What was he thinking? His body glowed under the bedclothes, hot with shame. If it hadn't been so absurdly funny, he would have cried. He, Jack Preston, on the best of terms with Enzo Ferrari? He had hoodwinked himself. It was all his own doing, his alone. He saw starlight through a chink in the curtains and threw off the sheets, unable to breathe.

In the kitchen he swallowed down a glass of water and looked through to the living room, lit up by the moon.

He saw the furniture – clumsy and nondescript – that cluttered the cottage.

He seemed to see it for the first time.

How could anyone have made these things without malice in mind?

They made him shudder.

65

Would the course of this story have been altered if Jack Preston had got wind of the photograph that Amélie Bonnard – a notary's daughter from a village in the foothills of the French Alps – had unknowingly taken at the moment when every press photographer was charging towards the royal box in the hope of capturing the spontaneous meeting between Deedee and the Prince? After 28 February 1969, it was a question that would always remain unanswered.

Three days previously, the lifeless body of Amélie Bonnard had been found by her husband at the foot of the white marble stairs at their villa in Cognac. Unable to endure the sight of her broken neck, he had slid his hand under her head and felt the fragments of her shattered skull move beneath his fingertips.

Amélie Bonnard had led a life of privilege; to be envied for her refinement had been her sole ambition. Her husband, whose name need not detain us, pursued his business interests with more luck than talent, a distinction rarely made in the circles in which he moved. But although he remains nameless here, his love for Amélie Bonnard was sincere and the tears he shed were of sorrow, not self-pity. Once his wife's father had solemnly read aloud her final wishes, it did not cross his mind for a second to disregard them by untying the bow and lifting the lid of the box of secrets with which she wished to be buried.

They were not exactly secrets, not all of them. The box contained letters. One from her grandfather to her grandmother, written in a dank and muddy trench, another from a Parisian girl, a friend from her youth. Both letters spoke of love: the former lofty and intense, the latter fresh and budding, ending with a proposal that Amélie Bonnard had continued to give thought to until the morning of her unfortunate fall. And of course there were photographs, many of them from her childhood, all showing Amélie in her Sunday best. Even the one photograph that did not feature her family had been taken on a Sunday. A snapshot from Monte Carlo.

It was an image that had never failed to move her. The piercing gaze of the unknown man in the red-and-gold overalls. His slicked hair blown forward by the rush of air. His arm reaching out to the delicate young girl. As if even now, in this photograph taken before the inferno, she was already safe.

66

In April, Cowe returned. One Sunday the bike Colin lent him when he worked on the farm was leaning against the wall outside the Black Swan. It appeared that the giant had spent the entire winter looking forward to another encounter with the burned car mechanic from Aldstead.

Jack Preston was a man of considerable willpower. As a boy he had begun to tinker with the engine of the old Massey Ferguson outside the shed and had kept on tinkering until, within a year or two, he had been able to provide for himself and his mother. The Lord had given him a modest talent and he had developed that talent with dogged determination. It was a trait that had led him to the British Rally Championships and ultimately to the Formula One circuit, achievements to which he and no-one else in Aldstead or Little Habton could lay claim. The steady swell of laughter in the Black Swan or outside the church after Mass did not goad him into a response. He was too proud to turn on them, none of them were worth it, no matter how their laughter pounded into him or how hollowly it echoed across the Mediterranean, in all those places he had been without ever belonging.

His impassiveness only made the laughter more

shameless, more wanton. On one occasion Maureen lashed out, but the silence that followed her outburst did not last long.

Later it occurred to him that impassiveness was a trait he shared with Ronny. And that this was one reason why it was so easy for Cowe and the others to reduce him to a kind of village idiot. He saw the inexorable process by which this happened and understood that it could happen to anyone at the same unsettling speed.

Maureen's pity choked him: her eagerness to stroke his head, every touch reminding him of his fate, left him feeling restless and desperate. But it was the realisation that he had begun to envy Ronny, who was at least happy and widely loved, that was the greatest humiliation of all.

67

At times it was stronger than he was, the desire for omnipotence, for retribution. The Avengers stirred their cups of tea in colourful cardboard sets designed to represent John Steed's stately bachelor pad, spouting theories about the motives of some villain whose evil scheme they were about to foil, and in the middle of these sparkling exchanges with their suggestive undertone – Steed never far from his bowler hat and brolly, Deedee usually draped across an armchair with legs poised playfully in mid air – Jack Preston would suddenly picture himself grabbing his coat and heading back to his workshop. Staring at the television screen, he saw himself crossing the street in the last light of the spring evening and climbing the path to the church as the bickering of the sparrows deep inside one of the cypresses settled into silence. He turned the key in the padlock, opened the door and took a deep breath, drinking in the smell of the familiar, a smell that strengthened his resolve. He knew precisely what he was looking for, knew by heart the place of every tool on the wall: even blindfolded he would be able to locate the smallest set of wire cutters. Standing at his workbench, he was struck by the weight of the moment, yet the last of his doubts disappeared as he slipped the cutters into his trouser pocket. Meanwhile Deedee and Steed jumped breezily into her open-topped sportscar and set off for the villain's grand country estate without a hint of trepidation. They drove through deserted landscapes and whizzed past manicured gardens, their clothes or the colours or perhaps their mere presence in the open air making it seem like they were on another planet. On his television screen Jack watched them speeding along and saw himself behind the wheel, the Cortina as hungry as ever, and as long as he was in the Cortina, he did not feel like a man abroad – not on the ferry, nor on his journey through the French countryside. The francs in his inside pocket were left over from his last time in Monaco, the place to which, according to the magazines that lay contritely at the far end of the dining table, Deedee had returned a few weeks earlier at the end of shooting, the series in the can. Yes, it was stronger than he was, at times. He knew the M.G. as well as he knew his own Cortina. Stopping only twice along the way, he drove from the North Sea to the Mediterranean – he would not stay there, he would speak to no-one – and as Deedee and Steed pulled up at the villain's house and simply rang the doorbell, he found her red M.G. parked in the street and knew exactly what had to be done. She had lived enough, enough for an entire lifetime. It took no more than a second or two. His lighter fell from his hands and he accidentally kicked it under the M.G. Two seconds at most, he knew exactly where to cut. Then he revved up the Cortina and simply drove back to Aldstead. And by the time Deedee and Steed had brought their villain to justice, Steed whipping out a sword concealed in his brolly and Deedee unleashing a barrage of martial arts moves and eventually managing to recover her tiny toy-sized pistol from the floor and wrap everything up, smiling and immaculate, he had spread the tarpaulin back over the Cortina, returned the cutters to their place above the workbench and turned the key in the padlock.

68

One evening Deedee looked straight into his eyes.

Steed had disappeared without trace and she did not know whether he was alive or dead. Speechless, racked with doubt, she went into the bathroom, leaned against the washbasin and gazed into the mirror – straight into the camera's lens – for seconds on end.

Jack Preston sank his nails deep into the arm of the settee.

There was no need for her to speak.

She was entrusting something to him. To him alone. Her look was like a whisper in his ear.

She was asking his forgiveness; this was the conclusion he reached minutes later. He had heard right, he had seen it in her face.

From that moment he looked at "The Avengers" through different eyes. He began to see that it was only in the guise of Emma Peel that Deedee revealed her true feelings, showed who she really was.

With that knowledge came intimacy.

He had a front-row seat.

He had been expecting a single grand gesture, an expectation that had blinded him to a myriad of subtle signals, straight from the heart and meant for him alone.

Patient. He had to be patient and forgive her for putting him through this ordeal. But the mere fact that she was asking his forgiveness made it seem as though they were already together somewhere.

69

Soon he discovered more.

He saw right through her impetuous light-heartedness. The make-up, ever more thickly applied, revealed a truth that remained hidden to others.

Deedee was unhappy.

She came from a religious family and had grown up in the countryside: he saw this in her. It was going too far, too fast. He saw it in her face as she listened to Steed or waited for her cue, the slight tremor above her eyebrow. This was a humiliation. The catsuits, the miniskirts, it was disrespectful – however forthright Emma Peel was, however much she stood up for herself. It had gone too fast. He saw it as though he had been through it himself. No-one else could suspect this of Deedee, as she skipped and laughed and enjoyed to the fullest everything life brought her way.

It was all an act.

Jack Preston prayed for her.

She was a prisoner of her fame. Lonely. No-one knew her by her real name anymore. It was clear to him that she longed for the life she had led before. Like him, she longed for Monte Carlo, the Monte Carlo that enthralled the senses, that promised you the world as it slipped through your fingers. She was sad and pretended to be so happy because she was sad. This was what he saw. She was choking on her own smokescreen. At heart she was still a simple girl. They were kindred spirits. Her exuberance was unnatural; he did not believe it. This was what he saw from his front-row seat.

Soon the charade would be at an end. It would all be over. It had begun with their embrace on boulevard Albert Premier, no-one since had given her that feeling. Her thoughts were with him, as his were with her. It would not be long in coming. Some things in life cannot remain without consequences.

MONTE CARLO

70

The darkness is not yet darkness. Not quite, not overhead.
The sky is a skin stretched tight, evenly lit in the palest and
most fragile of blues, so faint that nothing beneath it
remains illuminated. At most a contour can be traced – the
outline of the rise. The animals bow their heads and lower
their bodies to the ground. It is a July evening and the sky is
neither dark nor light and for miles around, from the village
to the medieval bridge, the only sound is the roar of four
raging cylinders under the bonnet of a Sutton Cortina. The
beam of the headlights slides low over the road, hugging the
tarmac between the thrashing branches of the wooded
banks. At this moment they exist alongside one another,
the beam, the darkness and the last of the light. Apollo 11
circles the moon. The Eagle has landed and Buzz Aldrin
unpacks a wafer and a small container of wine from his
pouch of personal belongings. Jack Preston takes the
bend, shifts into third gear, floors the accelerator and out
of the corner of his eye sees the gate to the meadow flash
past as he approaches the trees . . . Here the darkness
has become darkness and, high, very high above Aldstead,

Aldrin partakes of the sacrament of Holy Communion and invites each person listening on the radio to give thanks in his or her own way.

71

Many versions existed of the fateful event that occurred in Monte Carlo early in the morning of May 12, 1969. A chilly morning, wintry cold. Photographers from the news agencies and the local papers were quick to appear on the scene, countless rolls of film were shot, but not a single photograph would bring enlightenment, to say nothing of conclusive evidence.

The previous evening, Deedee had been spotted at a restaurant with the Princess. By all accounts it was highly unusual for the Princess to dine in public, yet it was common knowledge that she, though by no means old herself of course, had been like a mother to Deedee. Following last year's Grand Prix, far warmer ties with the royal household had swiftly been established. The Prince had not missed an opportunity to sing the praises of the young film star, and the publication of a grainy photograph of Deedee, sunbathing on the deck of a yacht with her hand apparently resting on the hand of a man who bore a physical resemblance to the Prince, had caused quite a stir, at least in the gossip columns.

The scene of the accident was high above the city; Deedee had plunged into the ravine. The first photographers had seen the flames from a distance but no-one had found a way to approach the wreckage and so everyone congregated at the mangled crash barrier.

It was later assumed that, at the time of the accident or perhaps after her precipitous fall, Deedee had lost consciousness and had probably not survived the impact on the rocks below. The possibility that she had been burned alive in her M.G. before the eyes of the assembled press was too unbearable for the world to contemplate.

One man was unable to contain himself and decided to attempt a descent. Marcel Toussaint of Fréjus stepped impulsively over the barrier and began to scramble down the steep incline. No sooner had he begun than he lost his footing and slid a good eight or nine feet into the ravine. Realising that his life was at risk and too afraid to climb back up, he sat like a little boy on a rocky outcrop until the emergency services came to rescue him.

From his perch, he, unlike his colleagues, had an unobstructed view of the horrific scene below and it was his photograph that circled the globe the next day. A striking whim of the mistral and the pattern of the flames had shaped the core of the blaze into a frayed and elongated heart that glowed bright orange in the dawn's early light.

The wealth and success that were the hallmarks of Marcel Toussaint's subsequent career as a photographer would always be tarnished by shame. Never, not even to his wife, did he confide the details of the fortunate accident that had befallen him in his position of utter helplessness. Many years later, as an elderly widower, when the winter sun shone directly into his room and often after eating the North-African casserole that was a regular fixture on the menu, a dish that well into the evening laced his mouth with the memory of the *pain d'épices* he had loved as a schoolboy, he let the tears roll down his cheeks as he shared the silence with his only granddaughter. The apple of her grandfather's eye, she never thought to ask him why he was crying.

72

One hour and twelve minutes. That was the length of time mentioned frequently in the days that followed. In any case it had taken the fire fighters more than an hour to reach the site of the accident and to find the smouldering wreckage of the burned-out car deep in the ravine. It was another fifteen minutes before the police arrived.

The fact that someone had taken the trouble to mobilise a pack of journalists so soon after the accident yet had failed to notify the emergency services was an immediate source of speculation.

In itself, the car's flashing indicator proved nothing.

Once the fire had run its course, someone noticed that the indicator nearest the ground, unharmed by the blaze, was flashing. It was a harrowing and ever more unbearable detail for those who stood looking down from the side of the road. For a short time, some had seen it as a sign that Deedee was still alive, that there was still hope.

73

No-one paid much credence to the theory that this was a crime of passion.

Since her tempestuous affair with a Portuguese shipping magnate, no photographer had captured her walking arm in arm with a man. It was virtually impossible for someone to have murdered Deedee, put her body behind the wheel of her M.G. and pushed her into the ravine; the mangled metal of the crash barrier suggested a collision at considerable speed.

More to the point, why would the killer have contacted the press so quickly? What purpose could that possibly serve?

Sabotage presented a more plausible line of inquiry.

The analogy with a pyromaniac seemed to pass muster. Just as a fire raiser cannot resist the temptation to admire his handiwork, this twisted mind might have been driven by a perverse thirst for glory. He had done what no-one else had dared even to consider. And he had done it to Deedee. The simple fact of her fame had sufficed. He had wanted as many witnesses as possible.

Newspaper staff pored over the photographs of the crash barrier and the fatal bend, studying the faces of the people gathered there. The chance that one of those faces might belong to Deedee's killer was thought to be realistic.

Flicking through their post, editors-in-chief secretly hoped that they would be the one to find a letter from the psychopath, taking credit for the crime in a childish scrawl or in words clipped letter by letter from newspaper headlines or perhaps even in crisp paragraphs of typescript, and concluding with a formal expression of the author's deepest respect.

The most painful theory was that this had been an act of desperation.

So painful it was almost taboo.

Not due to the raw fact of suicide, but due to the further implications. It would have meant that Deedee had planned everything and had herself tipped off the press in order to add lustre to the event, to ensure that its drama was recorded for posterity. A member of staff at her hotel had seen her emerge from the restaurant bar in the early hours of that morning, clearly intoxicated, and disappear into one of the telephone booths in the lobby.

This was not the Deedee people knew. She was most certainly unpredictable, but she was also modest. Deedee would never have flaunted her own despair in such a way.

It was unthinkable.

An unthinkable betrayal.

74

The police issued an official statement.

An expert investigation had produced evidence of skid marks on the road. No photographer had managed to capture them on film, yet it appeared that they had been there all along. It was a revelation that consigned a stack of scenarios to the wastepaper basket at a single stroke. The official record decreed that Deedee's demise had in all likelihood been the result of a road accident.

Within a day, a new official statement was released. The person who had witnessed the accident – it was unclear whether this was a man or a woman – and who had unwittingly called the press and subsequently a news agency, had now contacted the police and was helping them with their inquiries. The witness wished to remain anonymous and the police were prepared to grant this request on condition that no criminal offences had been committed. This served to reinforce the assertion that a road accident had taken place.

It did nothing to alter the facts or to ease the sorrow.

Deedee was dead.

Her body consumed by flames in her own car.

Deedee.

No-one at the scene of the accident would forget having been there.

The morning chill and the heat that rose from the depths.

The flashing indicator.

The birds.

Birdsong that rose suddenly from the bushes and trees in the ravine below. How, after a while, everyone stopped talking and taking photographs, and looked around in astonishment as they listened to the thrilling exuberance of the birds celebrating the return of the light, an angelic choir to sing Deedee to her rest.

75

Jack Preston was a man of thirty-six, his brilliantined hair combed back from his forehead, his sideburns a little longer than they had been the year before. It was ten o'clock in Aldstead on the morning of May 12. He clambered out of the oil pit in a state of bewilderment and walked over to the radio above his workbench to hear the news more clearly. He looked through the window at the ripening corn and listened to the voice from out at sea breaking the news of Deedee's death. His face betrayed no reaction, he listened. The news bulletin ended, his daze continued. He heard The Kinks, they sang of love. He sat on the ground with his back against the wall. He had never seen his workshop from this angle before. He counted the years. He smoked. At midday he ate half his lunch. He heard laughter, infectious laughter. It was his own. He had not killed her, yet he felt like a murderer, at the very least an accessory. What he had imagined had become reality. How could this be? He swallowed the tears that were welling inside him.

Shortly after two he heard the rattling of Maureen's bicycle. She stood in the doorway and asked if he had heard the news. He said yes and turned his back on her. A few minutes later he heard the rattling fade into the distance. He held a heavy spanner in his white-knuckled fist. He thought of his mother and his father. He saw the soldier standing at the front door, buttons gleaming, cap in hand, staring at a point above their heads. He felt his mother's hand clutch his as she braced herself for the blow from which she would never recover. He felt betrayed. After all this time, God had taken his side. His prayers had been answered. But he had not been rewarded for his sacrifice in Monte Carlo; Deedee had been punished for her negligence.

76

On Sunday, May 18, shortly before the start of the Formula One Grand Prix, a minute's silence was held in memory of Deedee, who had been laid to rest in Paris the previous day. It was a minute the Prince had been dreading for three days. His personal physician had slipped him a pill that, while it numbed the pain, also left him feeling faint-hearted. The memories from one year earlier were still vivid. It seemed only yesterday that he had held Deedee in his arms after her miraculous escape, on the same platform where her lonely portrait now stood, black crepe draped over one corner. There was no escape from the cameras. Everyone wanted to see his face, his wife's face, and what might be read in their expressions. He had put on a pair of dark glasses though the sky this afternoon was overcast, the summit of Monte Carlo lost in cloud.

When the throng around the circuit, almost a quarter of a million people, fell silent and an unprecedented hush settled on his principality, it was difficult for him to relax his face, to breathe, to stay on his feet. It overwhelmed him. Photographers grew ashamed of the greedy clicks of their shutters and within twenty seconds they had all lowered their cameras in a show of respect.

People fixed their eyes on the asphalt or on a building; they did not look at one another.

A ship's horn sounded far out to sea.

The television cameras kept rolling, alternating between images of the royal family and the drivers and team bosses, who had stepped forward to form an informal guard of honour along the starting line. Some clasped their hands, most stood with their arms crossed.

There was no applause when the minute ended. No sign was given. Sixty seconds had long passed before the first people began to look around and make the first tentative movements, and slowly the rest followed. The Prince turned to his wife and both of them sat down on the high-backed chairs, slowly, as if deadened by fatigue.

Through the legs of the line-up, Jack Preston saw Howard's blue Matra in pole position. The differences in the drivers' race suits and in the advertising had already caught his eye. The short fins on either side of the Matra's nose made it look strangely shark-like. Later he saw Gill put on his helmet, a new design that protected the entire face and gave him the sinister aspect of a Roman gladiator rather than a British racing driver.

The camera zoomed in on Deedee's portrait one last time before the tripod was removed from the platform. It was a profile shot, taken on a summer's day. Deedee did not seem to be aware of the photographer, despite the proximity at which the picture had been taken. She was lost in thought and a soft, wide hat sheltered her from the glaring sun, which shone through little holes in the brim and scattered bright diamonds across her face. The photograph had been taken a few years earlier and it seemed now as if, sensing what fate had in store, she was pausing for an instant in the shade before looking up with a smile and striding forward to face the madness.

77

On the moon, the earth rose, three-quarters illuminated by the sun. The light and heat forced their way through the unsightly atmosphere and reached the body of Maureen Coxwold on a beach not far from Aldstead. A couple of hours later she cycled to her husband's workshop, charged with emotion. She did not wait in the doorway but said hello and walked straight in, and seeing that Ronny was not around, she stepped out of her summer dress. She stood directly in front of him and felt the heat that she was giving off in the coolness of this space. She placed his hand on her breast and closed her eyes. Two months and two days had passed since the Grand Prix in Monaco, and more than once Maureen had run her hands over the back of his head but only now did Jack Preston respond. Time had slipped by unnoticed, she had touched him, in bed, in the living room, and he had felt nothing. Now he felt like an animal, cornered by the thought of her hands stroking his scars again, pity from the daughter of a building contractor from Little Habton. With all his might, he pushed her away from him. He saw what he was doing, pushing hard with both arms. He saw her fall to the ground in front of his work-bench, more naked than she had ever been. Music played on the radio and her hands reached out behind her as she fell. He saw the jolt as her body hit the ground, the physical impact. His wife lay naked before him on the dirt floor, helpless, yet the fall had not ended. Its momentum turned into a crawling motion as she scrambled away from him. In a protective gesture she gathered her breasts to her in one arm while her other hand groped for her white summer dress.

78

Jack Preston had barely moved when, perhaps an hour later, Ronny walked into the workshop, feet dragging. The boy was feeling the heat. Sweat beaded on his forehead and along the broad white parting in his black hair. He was wearing the clothes he always wore. His thick tongue rested on his lower lip and towards the back it seemed to be plastered with a layer of whitish-yellow. He approached Jack Preston, came within a few feet, panting slightly, shoulders hunched, arms hanging low. He had the air of a grazing animal that had wandered over out of sheer boredom and was standing next to him as if he were not even there. Jack felt he was being mocked somehow, humiliated. Why Deedee, a glorious, gifted young woman? Why not this insignificant boy from the back of beyond? Why should Ronny be spared, cherished like a precious stone? And why did the Lord keep sending the boy to him?

It was as if God were mocking him.

He felt betrayed. Betrayed and mocked.

79

Jack Preston did not move. This took Ronny by surprise, made him feel uncertain. He lowered his eyes and waited to see what would happen. They stood together in the workshop and Jack said nothing. He showed no sign of going back to work, nor did he give Ronny permission to sit in one of the cars. Music came from the radio, one song after another. After a while, Ronny decided to take the chance; Jack was not working, they were still standing close together and so he said it.

"Cortina."

Jack did not seem to hear.

"Drive Cortina."

"There's no balance."

As their eyes met, Jack said these words again.

"No . . . b-balance," echoed Ronny, forcing the last word out. He shook his head as if he deplored this state of affairs more than Jack himself. He sounded angry.

A change washed across Jack's face; Ronny responded instantly with a broad grin. Jack turned to the boy and told him what an ugly little sod he was. Ronny doubled up in a show of hilarity.

"You and me both."

"Yes," Ronny said eagerly, looking up at the ceiling. "No b-balance!"

Jack Preston's eyes grew distant once again.

A little while later he got back to work and soon the afternoon began to resemble yesterday afternoon and all the afternoons before. As he rummaged around for a spare part in the drawers of his workbench, Ronny came and stood next to him. He asked the boy if he could count. If he could count to ten.

Ronny shook his head. "Twenty!"

"Will you count to twenty for me?"

The boy sang. Without a moment's hesitation, he sang his way to twenty.

Jack Preston said it was the finest bit of counting he had ever heard.

Then he asked the boy if he believed in God.

"Jesus," Ronny said.

"And you believe in Jesus?"

"Baby Jesus."

"Baby Jesus?"

"Yeah," the boy answered happily. "Ronny."

Jack Preston said in that case they had better go to church and light a candle. He asked the boy if he would count to four when they got there, because that was the number they needed. They were going to light four candles. Ronny nodded emphatically.

In the shadow of one of the cypresses, he let the boy take the last draw of his cigarette. The air in the wooden porch was treacle thick. Unsure of his steps or his sight, Ronny bowed his head stiffly to look at the worn doorstep. Jack knelt in the front pew, the boy imitated all his gestures.

"You tell it," Jack Preston said, when they walked into the kitchen of the cottage. Maureen took Ronny's hands in hers and listened patiently as the boy explained how he had lit the candles in the church. Four candles. Two for his mother and father, and two for Jack's mother and father. Four. He repeated the number as if it were the answer to a sum. Now he was hungry. He turned and sat down at the table.

Over by the sink, Jack Preston stood behind his wife and buried his face in her hair. While Ronny spontaneously sang his way to twenty, Jack whispered two sentences in her ear, words that meant nothing to anyone but Maureen Coxwold, words she would never forget, for she had first heard them in the darkness behind the Black Swan on the night they met.

Jack said they still had work to do and Ronny ate as they walked. Traces of his sandwich around his open mouth, the boy was speechless when Jack said he had a surprise in store, walked to the back of the workshop and whipped the tarpaulin off the Cortina.

"She can give the Apollo a run for her money."

There was so much Ronny wanted to say, but the first word blocked the way for the rest. Overcome with excitement, his face turned bright red. Jack told him to calm down, that there was no need for him to speak.

He put his arms around the boy.

"There now, calm down."

He felt the tension ebb from the boy's short, crudely assembled frame.

"Save your strength. I need your help."

A few minutes later they had rolled the Cortina over the oil pit and a motionless, shining stripe of waste oil drained into the drum.

"God watches over us, Ronny. You know that, don't you?"

"Yes."

"God watches over us."

Ronny nodded. "Baby Jesus."

"And children most of all. Did you know that?"

"Yes."

Jack Preston turned the screw back into the crankcase and Ronny handed him the fresh can of oil that he had been allowed to tap from the drum himself.

"Children like you."

"Ronny."

"Yes. Ronny. He's very fond of you."

The boy tapped himself on the chest. "Ronny . . ."

"But first we're going to polish the Cortina. Fetch us the shammies, will you?"

They polished the car with circular motions until they were both out of breath and had no strength left in their arms.

The bodywork shone.

"We're in good hands," Jack Preston said. "He will show us the way. He has to. He loves His Ronny."

"Yes," the boy said. "Baby Jesus."

"Will you count for me in a little while?"

"Twenty!"

"I'll tell you when."

Ronny looked at him.

"Soon. Over by the trees."

"Yes."

"And then you can do your best counting ever."

"Yes," Ronny said, scrunching up his eyes.

They pushed the Cortina through the doorway and into the open air. The darkness was not yet darkness. Not quite. The engine growled into life and the boy shouted at the top of his lungs, clapping his hands, rocking with happiness in the seat next to Jack Preston.

80

Dawn raced from east to west, a sharp line that swept across the map of the United States and triggered an explosion of shortwave radio traffic in the course of the British afternoon. Blunt had been rooted to the spot since two, listening intently to the receiver through his headphones. The Black Swan would still be standing tomorrow and if the woman he had been waiting for all his life decided to turn up in Aldstead today, she clearly wasn't the one for him after all.

The excitement among radio hams had reached fever pitch. It was rumoured that an amateur from Louisville,

Kentucky, had picked up on the "local" communication between Aldrin in the Eagle and Collins in Apollo 11, a fainter signal on different frequencies to the transmissions between Apollo 11 and Mission Control in Houston, which were encoded to prevent Soviet interception. The Louisville ham was said to be planning to broadcast the recordings he had made, and speculation was rife as to which wavelength he would use. Blunt concentrated in an effort to filter the many voices in the ether. Crumbs on the plate beside his camouflage-green radio told him he had already eaten.

After listening for hours on end, ears burning, he decided to step outside for a breath of fresh air. He gazed up at the pylon and the antenna anchored to the earth in concrete. The pointed metal construction was black against the evening sky. He walked around to the front of the house. The land that extended below him was bathed in darkness and the inky-blue dome high above him held a gleaming sickle. This mysterious apparition had taken up its place in the heavens long before there were eyes to see it. Then and there, it was as if the complete story of the landing hit him, beneath this endless sky, standing alone in the quiet of his own front garden.

A light moving through the darkness caught his eye, like a lantern being carried across the landscape in front of him. No, it was further away; he had misjudged the distance. It was a car. The hollow roads and wooded banks were being lit from below. He heard nothing, the wind at his back strong enough to keep the distant sound from reaching him. Unless his eyes were still deceiving him, the car was travelling at speed. As he pondered this thought, the light suddenly vanished, as if the driver had shut off his headlights. He waited for it to reappear. His gaze moved at the same speed, tracking the car's route across the hillside, but the light did not return.

Blunt turned his eyes skywards again. He smiled. How many people would be standing there like him right now, having stepped outside to look up? Alone in the quiet of their own front garden but together under the spell of the same moon. And, though they knew better, how many like him had tried to make out a tiny speck on the surface, from which a human being would appear, a man who would take one step and achieve immortality.

81

Early to bed, early to rise. It was a habit Norris maintained, though he could no longer call himself a farmer. He had not been asleep long when he was woken by a sound outside, over by the road. In his bleary state, the loud bang barely left a dent on his consciousness and he went straight back to sleep. The waking had been so brief that Norris had forgotten it by morning.

He splashed water on his face, pulled on his smock and walked out into the yard in his Wellington boots. The new day was glowing above the land down by the river. In another hour, at about five, the sun would light up the corn. The quiet and the beauty and the simplicity: a gift for those with eyes to see and ears to hear. Six years now since Norris had been forced to sell the land to Colin, yet he still looked at the fields around his house as if they were his own. He was the only one looking at them. In those first hours before breakfast with his wife, it was as if nothing had changed.

The few remaining animals were no reason for Norris to get up this early. He mucked out the stable, milked the cows and watched the waving corn and the glinting sun. And when at last he went back into the house to make breakfast, it was with the feeling that he had stolen a march on the rest of the world. That the day, whatever it might bring, had already been worth living.

At six-thirty on the dot, having set the table and squeezed the orange juice, Norris lifted his wife from her bed in the living room and lowered her into the wheelchair; by six-thirty her medicine had worn off. He provided a running commentary, detailing what he was doing with her, what he was about to do and what he had already done. His wife did not say a word. In the bathroom he pulled her nightie off over her head, placed her arms around his neck and straightened up to lift her from the chair. He washed her. Once her back was done he left the room and, sitting on a towel, she did the front herself.

At the table, his wife faced the window and Norris fetched and carried for her. They ate breakfast in the order that had become their own with the steady passing of the years. The door was open and the cooing of turtledoves filled the kitchen. Then they heard another sound out in the yard. It came from the front of the house and echoed off the stable wall and into the kitchen at the back. A voice they would know anywhere. Norris turned to look at the clock above the fire. Five to seven. There was a moment of doubt. Ronny never came to see them before eight. Never. He heard the voice again, still coming from out front, hoarser than usual, angry too, as if he were giving himself a thorough telling off as he sat there in the grass.

"Ronny's here," his wife said.

Norris cleared a space on the table and fetched the towel and the horn comb from the cupboard. He was looking forward to the ritual, come early this morning: his wife taking the boy on her lap, knotting the towel around his neck and combing his raven black hair for far longer than necessary. How her face, her mouth, would soften and he would once again glimpse the woman he had loved for so long. And how together they would watch as, solemnly and a little stiff in the neck, Ronny would walk over to the mirror above the sink and, too early, anticipating his reflection, he would say in one flowing sentence: Ronny is a handsome lad. How they would watch as he stood motion-less and smiling, and his face became a medieval portrait that filled the frame of the mirror. And suddenly, with no goodbye, without another word, he would be off out the door. Where to . . . God only knew.

Thanks to the Dutch Foundation for Literature for my stay at the writer's residence in Amsterdam and to the Flemish Literature Fund for a travel grant to visit Yorkshire. Many thanks to Suzanne and Henk and everyone at De Bezige Bij. Special thanks to Valeria, my wife.

PETER TERRIN has earned comparisons with such writers as Franz Kafka and Albert Camus. *The Guard* (2012) won him the European Union Literature Prize, and for *Post Mortem* (2015) he was awarded the prestigious A.K.O. Literature Prize. His work has been translated into many languages.

DAVID DOHERTY studied English and literary linguistics in Glasgow before moving to Amsterdam, where he has been working as a translator for the past twenty years. His translations include novels by critically acclaimed Dutch authors Marente de Moor, Jaap Robben and Hanneke Hendrix.